THE ONLY LIVING BOY

ONCE UPON A TIME

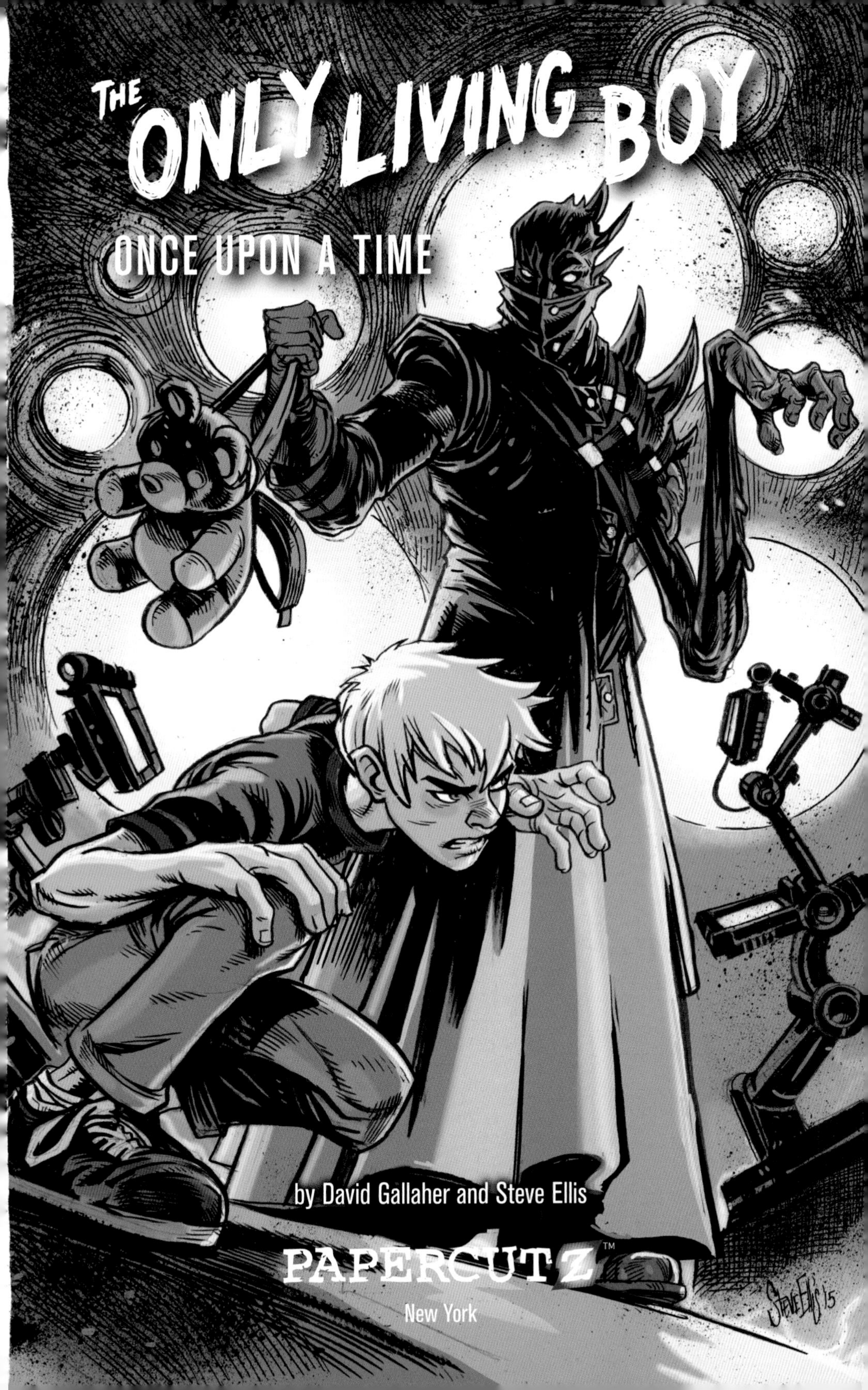

by David Gallaher and Steve Ellis

PAPERCUTZ™
New York

To my friend Carol, for comics and social justice.
– David

For my children, Jacob and Luna;
my art is a love song to you both.
– Steve

THE ONLY LIVING BOY #3 "Once Upon a Time"

Chapters 5 and 6:
Writer/ Co-Creator: David Gallaher
Artist/ Co-Creator: Steve Ellis
Color Flatting: Holley McKend
Lettering: Melanie Ujomori
Consulting Editor: Janelle Asselin
Assistants: Emily Walton, Aryeal Jackson

Originally serialized at: www.the-only-living-boy.com

Papercutz books may be purchased for business or promotional use.
For information on bulk purchases please contact Macmillan Corporate and
Premium Sales Department at:
(800) 221-795 x5442.

Production – Dawn Guzzo
Cover Logo – Adam Grano
Production Coordinator – Brittanie Black
Assistant Managing Editor – Jeff Whitman
Jim Salicrup
Editor-in-Chief

PB ISBN: 978-1-62991-589-0
HC ISBN: 978-1-62991-590-6

Printed in China
October 2016 by O.G. Printing Productions, LTD.

Distributed by Macmillan
First Papercutz Printing

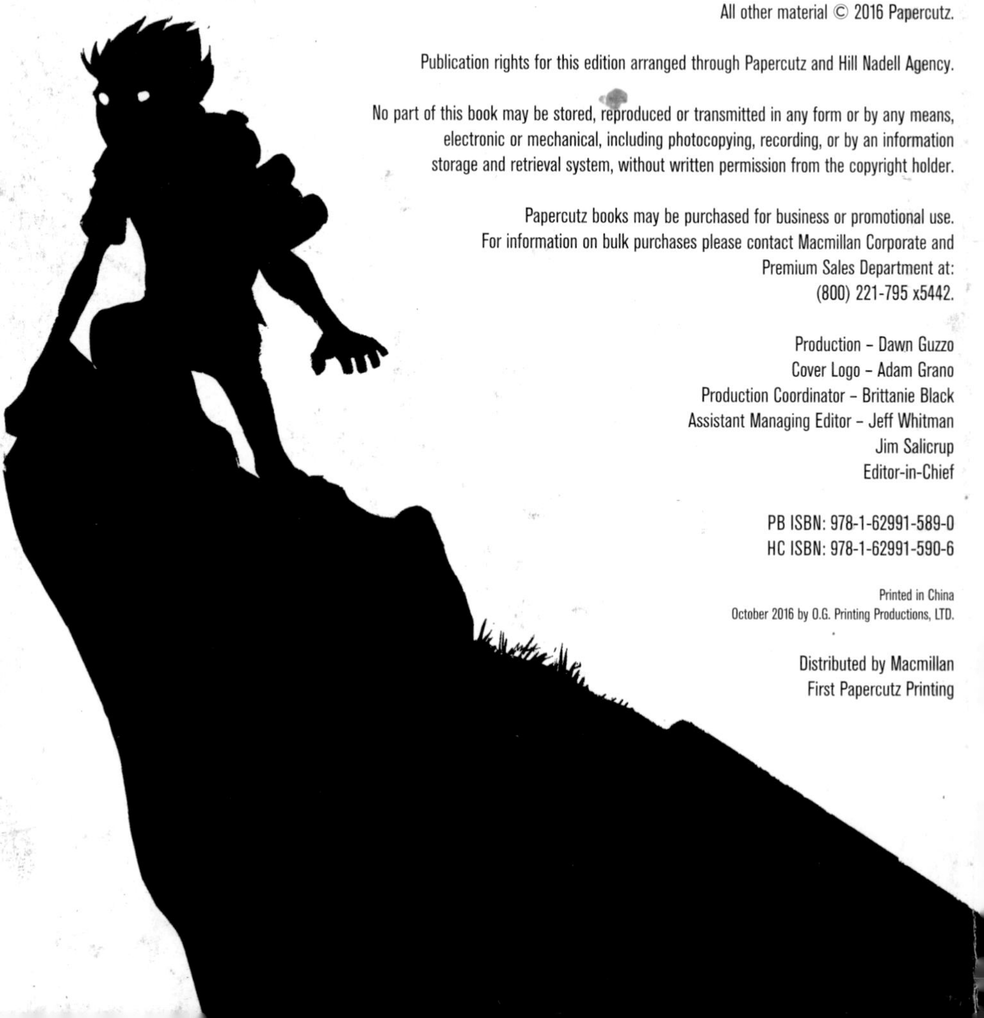

CHAPTER FIVE

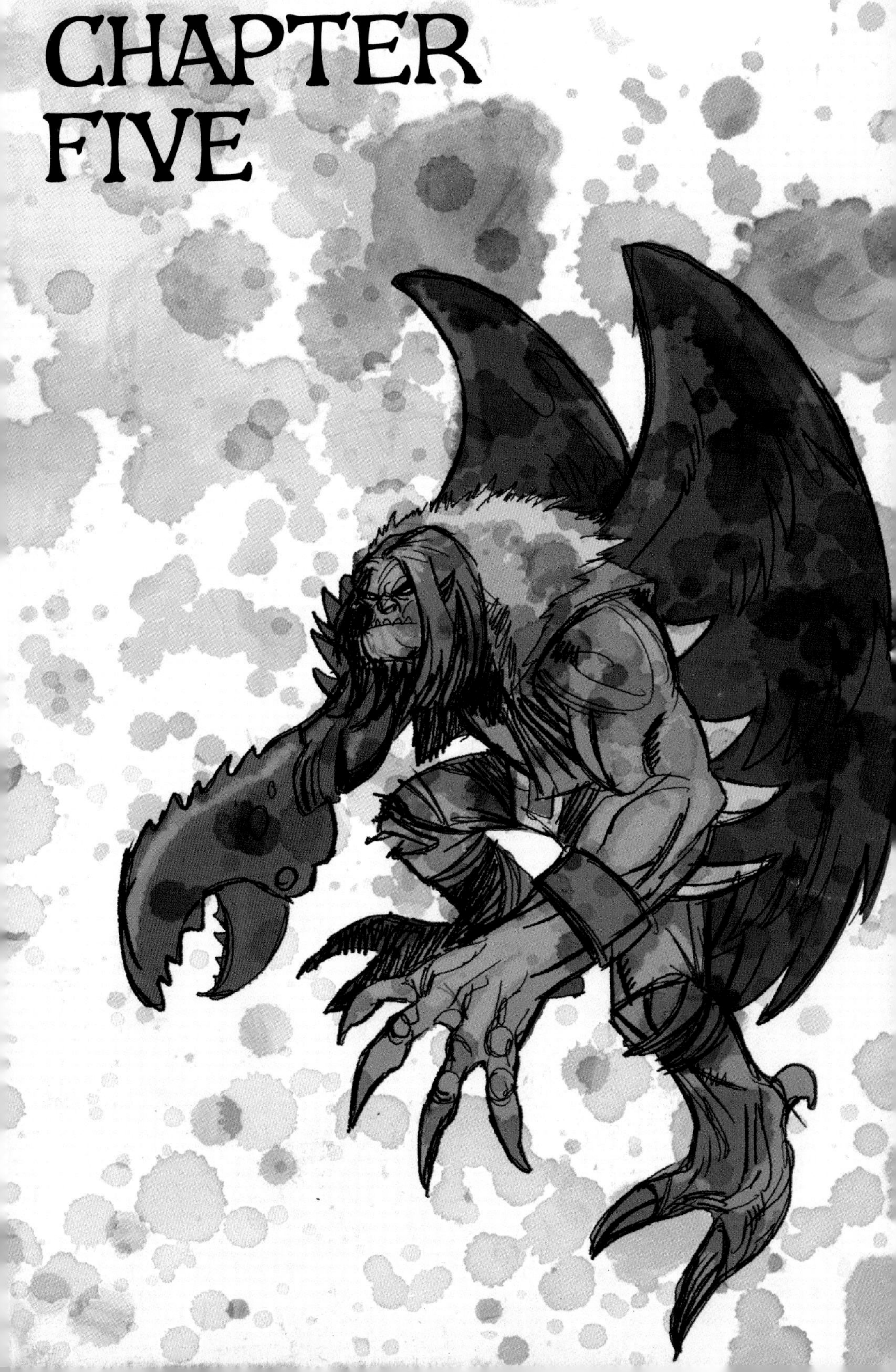

Previously in...

THE ONLY LIVING BOY

Twelve-year-old Erik Farrell continues his journey through a patchwork planet. After escaping the Groundling's city, Erik and his lucky medallion reunite with his friends Morgan and Thea. He convinces the Mermidonians to allow Thea to leave, even though her impending "Chrysalis" could threaten them all. Dodging monsters along the way, the friends make their way to Thea's flying city, Sectuarius. Thea's mother, the queen, says she can help restore Erik's memories. But just as he begins to see glimpses of the life he led, Doctor Once's minions attack and Erik and his friends must defend the Chrysalis chamber from his experiments. Erik fights hard, but soon he's falling through the clouds, until he wakes up in a place both familiar and alien...and finds his mother! Is Erik truly home?

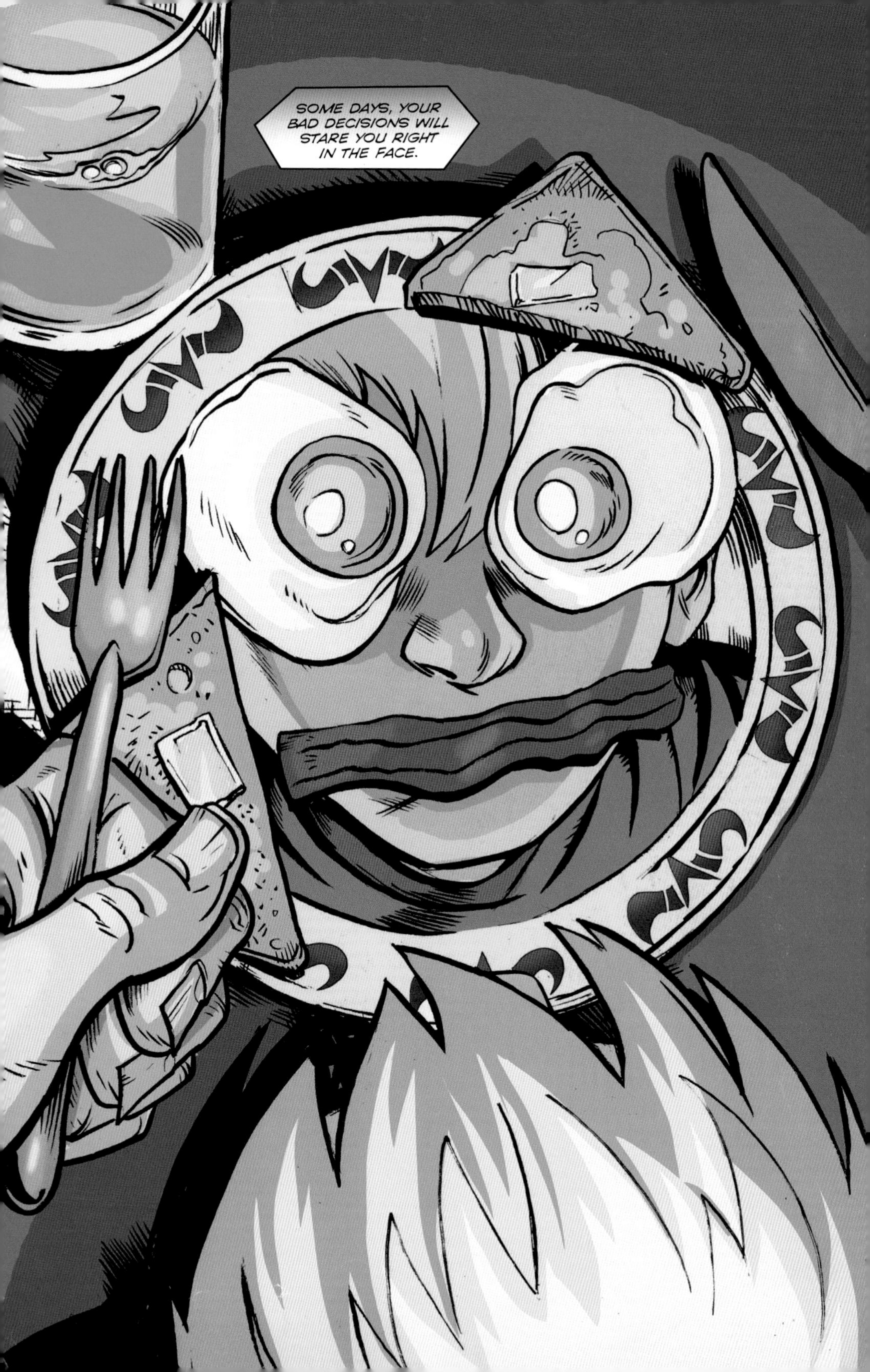
SOME DAYS, YOUR BAD DECISIONS WILL STARE YOU RIGHT IN THE FACE.

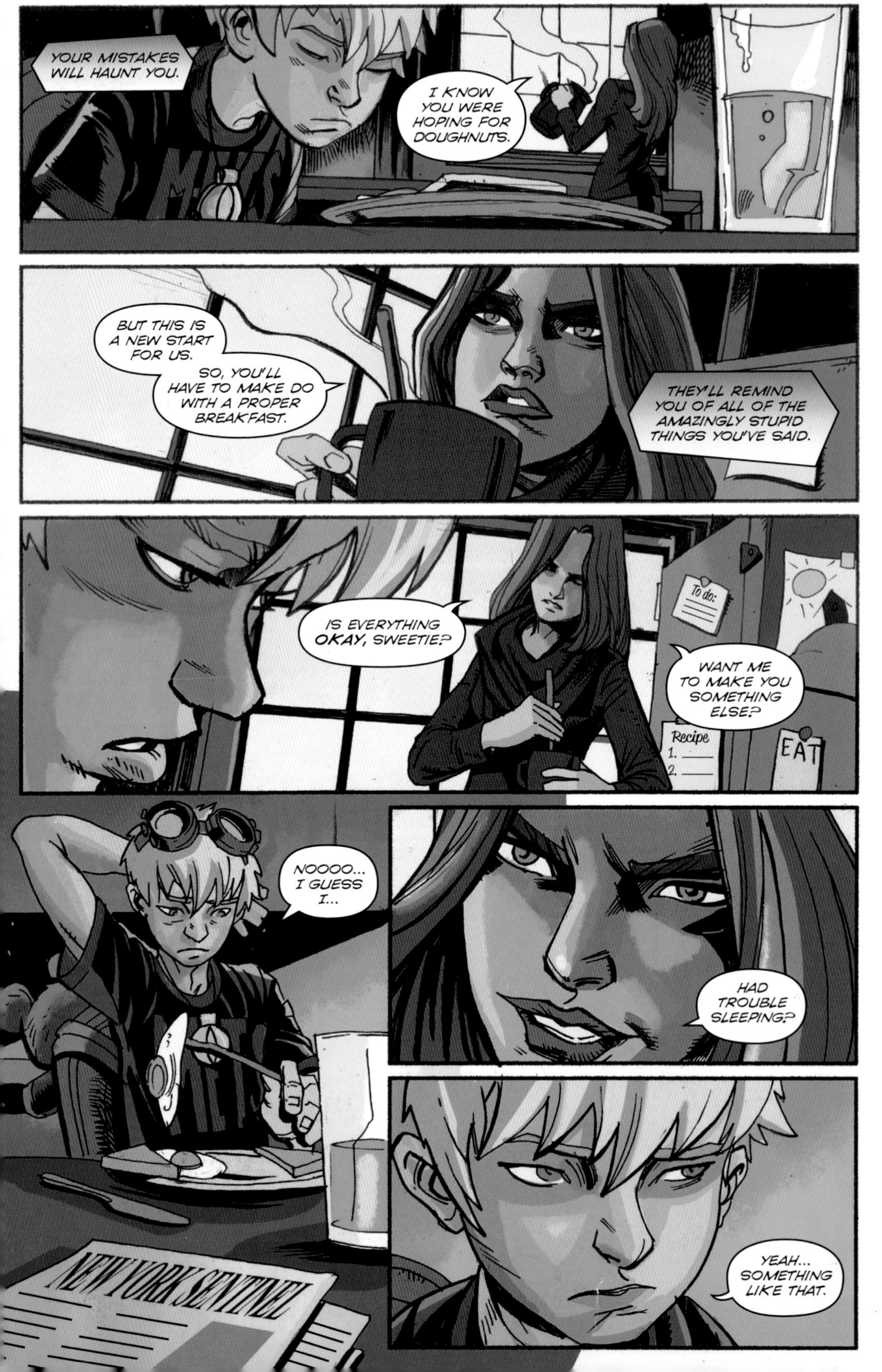
YOUR MISTAKES WILL HAUNT YOU.
I KNOW YOU WERE HOPING FOR DOUGHNUTS.
BUT THIS IS A NEW START FOR US.
SO, YOU'LL HAVE TO MAKE DO WITH A PROPER BREAKFAST.
THEY'LL REMIND YOU OF ALL OF THE AMAZINGLY STUPID THINGS YOU'VE SAID.
IS EVERYTHING OKAY, SWEETIE?
To do:
WANT ME TO MAKE YOU SOMETHING ELSE?
Recipe
1.
2.
EAT
NOOOO... I GUESS I...
HAD TROUBLE SLEEPING?
NEW YORK SENTINEL
YEAH... SOMETHING LIKE THAT.

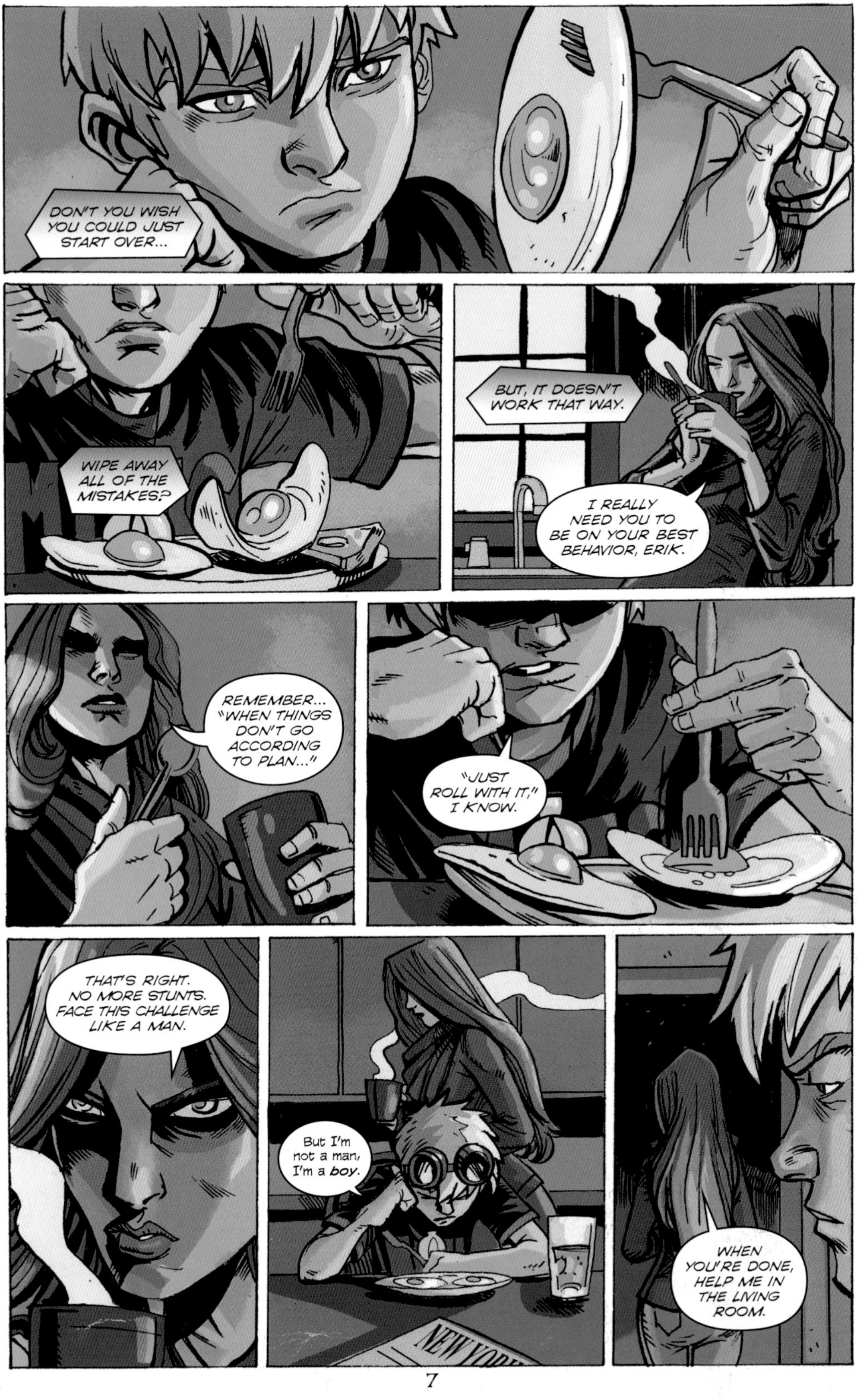
DON'T YOU WISH YOU COULD JUST START OVER...
WIPE AWAY ALL OF THE MISTAKES?
BUT, IT DOESN'T WORK THAT WAY.
I REALLY NEED YOU TO BE ON YOUR BEST BEHAVIOR, ERIK.
REMEMBER... "WHEN THINGS DON'T GO ACCORDING TO PLAN..."
"JUST ROLL WITH IT," I KNOW.
THAT'S RIGHT. NO MORE STUNTS. FACE THIS CHALLENGE LIKE A MAN.
But I'm not a man, I'm a *boy*.
WHEN YOU'RE DONE, HELP ME IN THE LIVING ROOM.

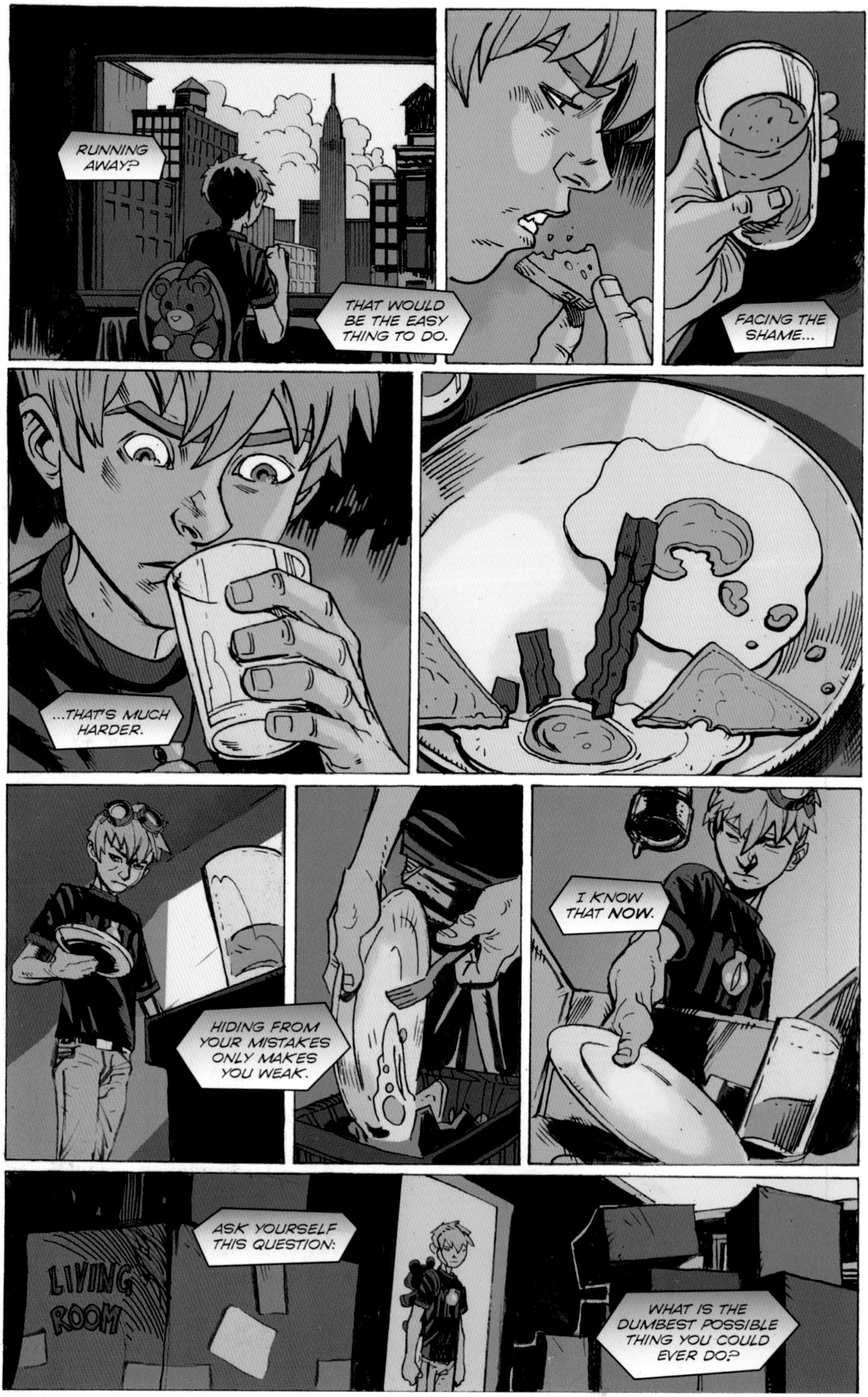
RUNNING AWAY?
THAT WOULD BE THE EASY THING TO DO.
FACING THE SHAME...
...THAT'S MUCH HARDER.
HIDING FROM YOUR MISTAKES ONLY MAKES YOU WEAK.
I KNOW THAT NOW.
ASK YOURSELF THIS QUESTION:
LIVING ROOM
WHAT IS THE DUMBEST POSSIBLE THING YOU COULD EVER DO?

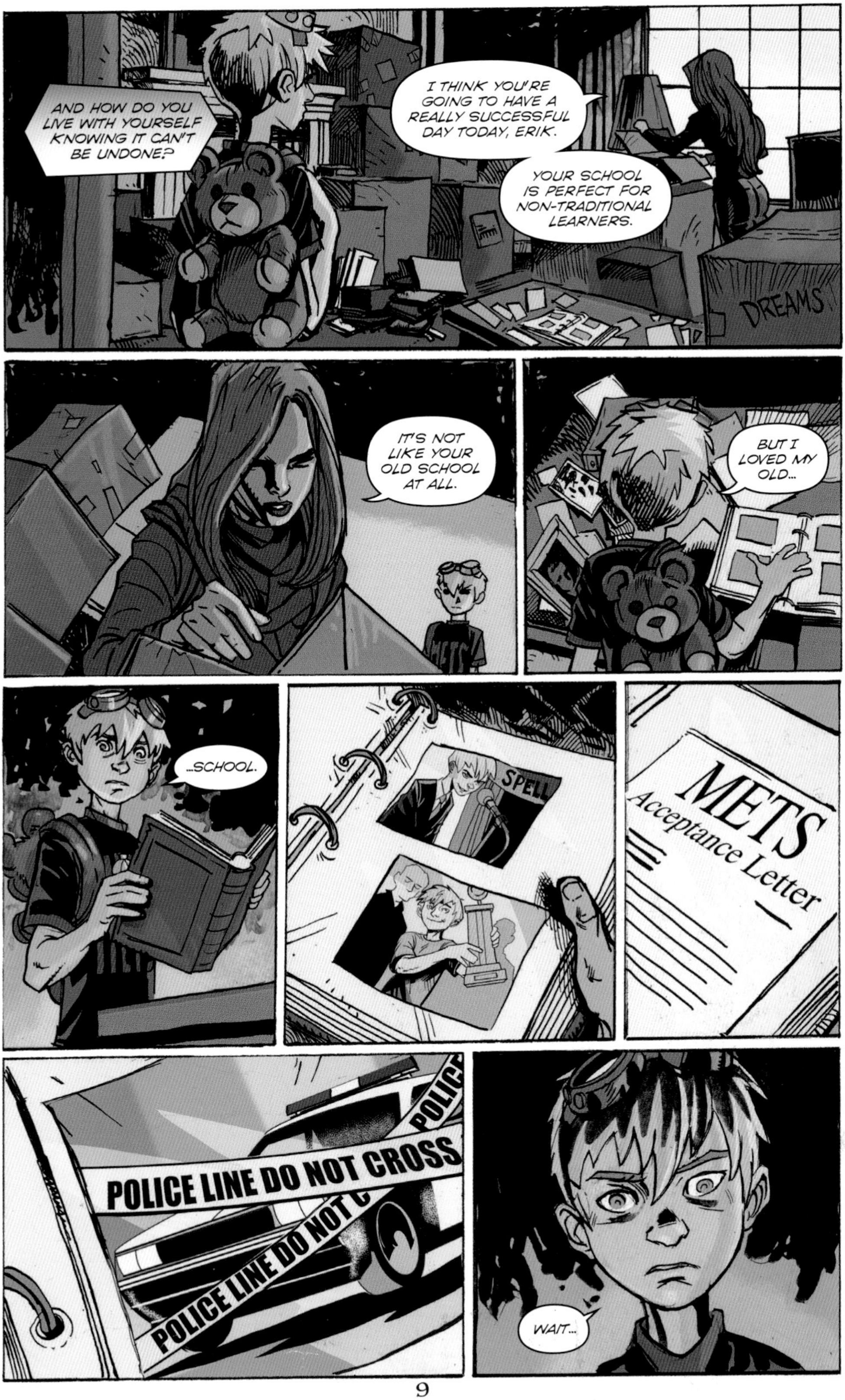
AND HOW DO YOU LIVE WITH YOURSELF KNOWING IT CAN'T BE UNDONE?
I THINK YOU'RE GOING TO HAVE A REALLY SUCCESSFUL DAY TODAY, ERIK.
YOUR SCHOOL IS PERFECT FOR NON-TRADITIONAL LEARNERS.
DREAMS
IT'S NOT LIKE YOUR OLD SCHOOL AT ALL.
BUT I LOVED MY OLD...
...SCHOOL.
SPELL
METS
Acceptance Letter
POLICE
POLICE LINE DO NOT CROSS
POLICE LINE DO NOT C
WAIT...

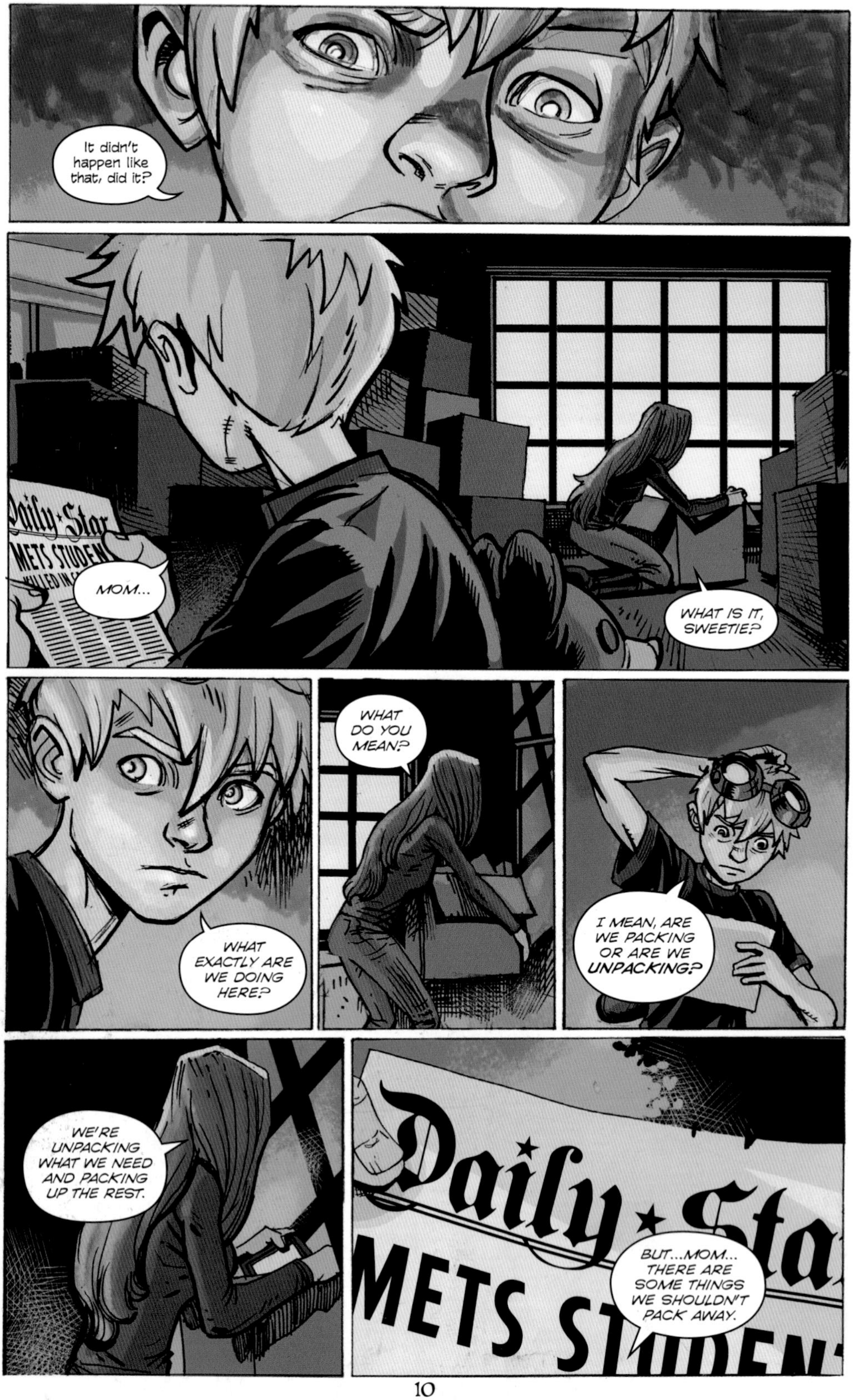
It didn't happen like that, did it?
Daily Star
METS STUDEN
MOM...
WHAT IS IT, SWEETIE?
WHAT EXACTLY ARE WE DOING HERE?
WHAT DO YOU MEAN?
I MEAN, ARE WE PACKING OR ARE WE UNPACKING?
WE'RE UNPACKING WHAT WE NEED AND PACKING UP THE REST.
BUT...MOM... THERE ARE SOME THINGS WE SHOULDN'T PACK AWAY.

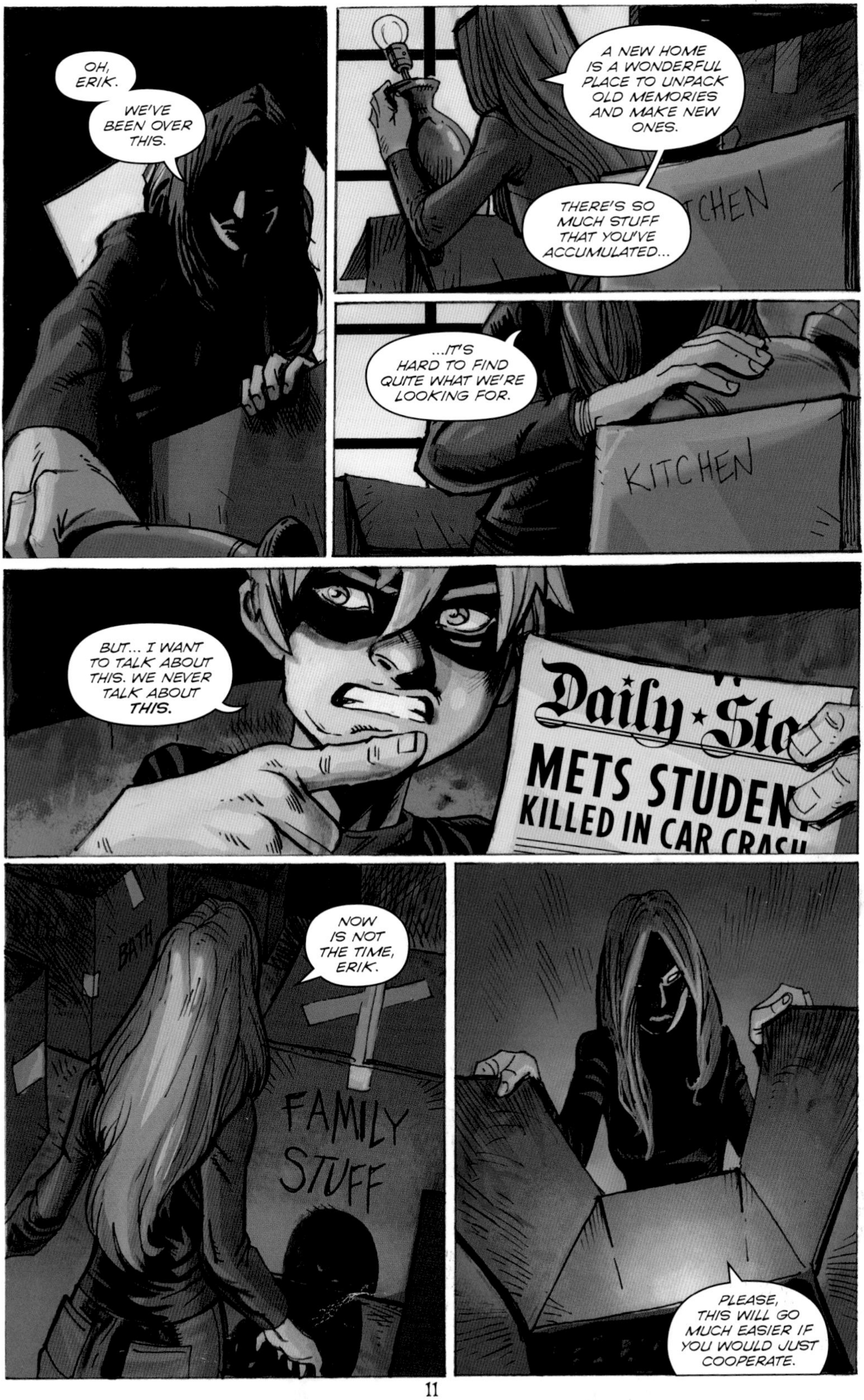
OH, ERIK.
WE'VE BEEN OVER THIS.
A NEW HOME IS A WONDERFUL PLACE TO UNPACK OLD MEMORIES AND MAKE NEW ONES.
THERE'S SO MUCH STUFF THAT YOU'VE ACCUMULATED...
KITCHEN
...IT'S HARD TO FIND QUITE WHAT WE'RE LOOKING FOR.
KITCHEN
BUT... I WANT TO TALK ABOUT THIS. WE NEVER TALK ABOUT THIS.
Daily Sta
METS STUDEN
KILLED IN CAR CRAS
BATH
NOW IS NOT THE TIME, ERIK.
FAMILY STUFF
PLEASE, THIS WILL GO MUCH EASIER IF YOU WOULD JUST COOPERATE.

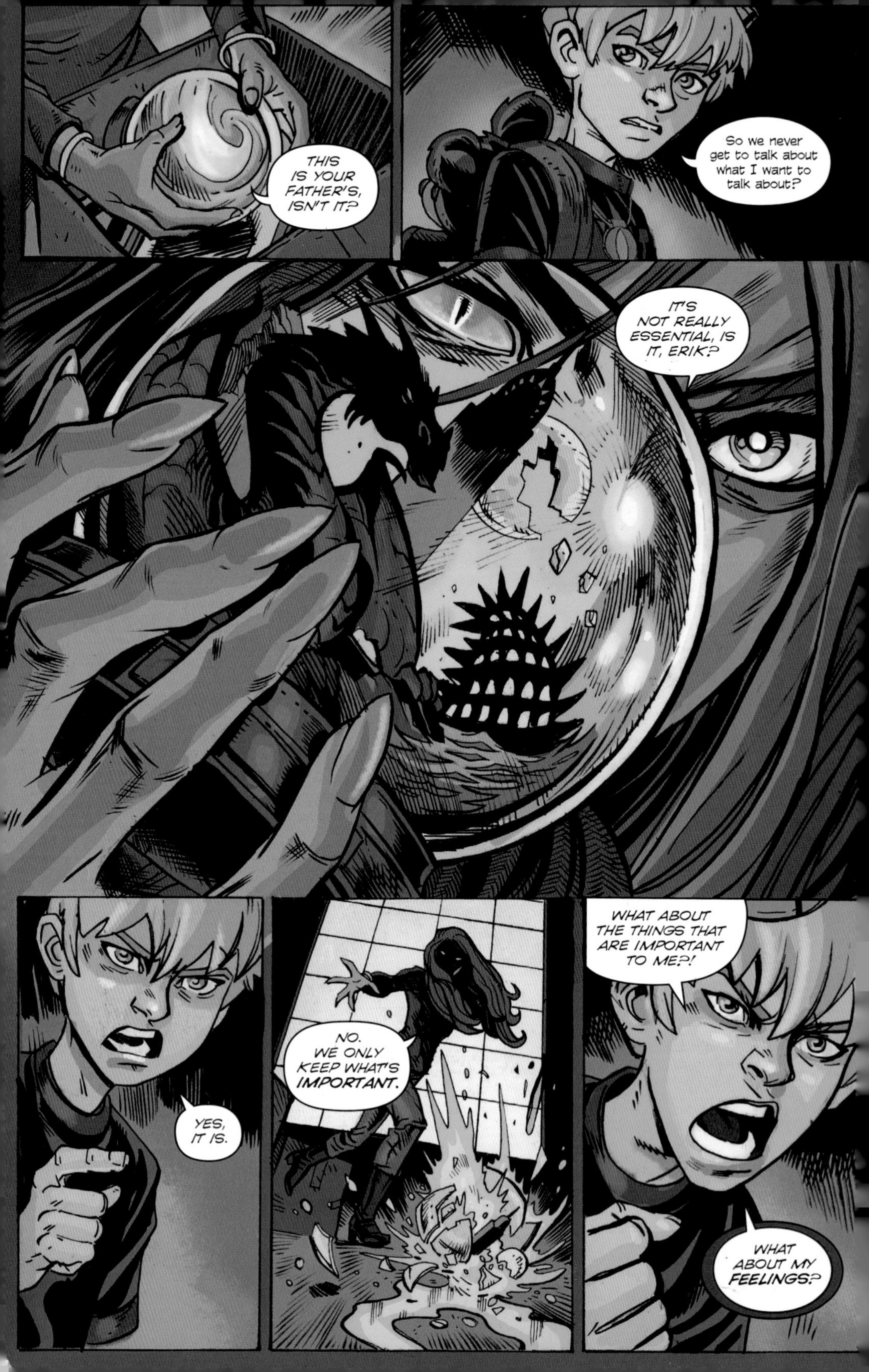
THIS IS YOUR FATHER'S, ISN'T IT?
So we never get to talk about what I want to talk about?
IT'S NOT REALLY ESSENTIAL, IS IT, ERIK?
YES, IT IS.
NO. WE ONLY KEEP WHAT'S IMPORTANT.
WHAT ABOUT THE THINGS THAT ARE IMPORTANT TO ME?!
WHAT ABOUT MY FEELINGS?

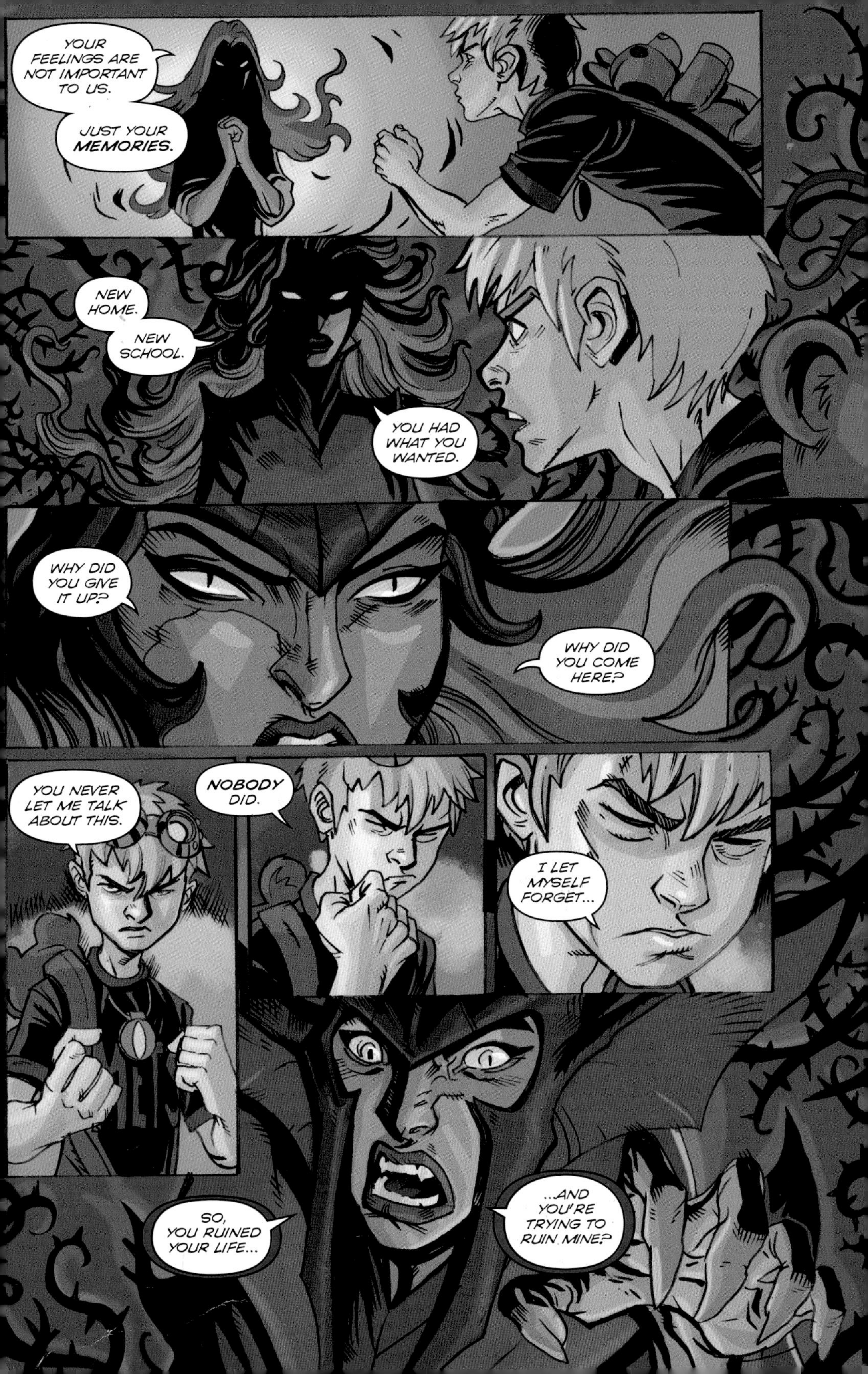
YOUR FEELINGS ARE NOT IMPORTANT TO US.
JUST YOUR MEMORIES.
NEW HOME.
NEW SCHOOL.
YOU HAD WHAT YOU WANTED.
WHY DID YOU GIVE IT UP?
WHY DID YOU COME HERE?
YOU NEVER LET ME TALK ABOUT THIS.
NOBODY DID.
I LET MYSELF FORGET...
SO, YOU RUINED YOUR LIFE...
...AND YOU'RE TRYING TO RUIN MINE?

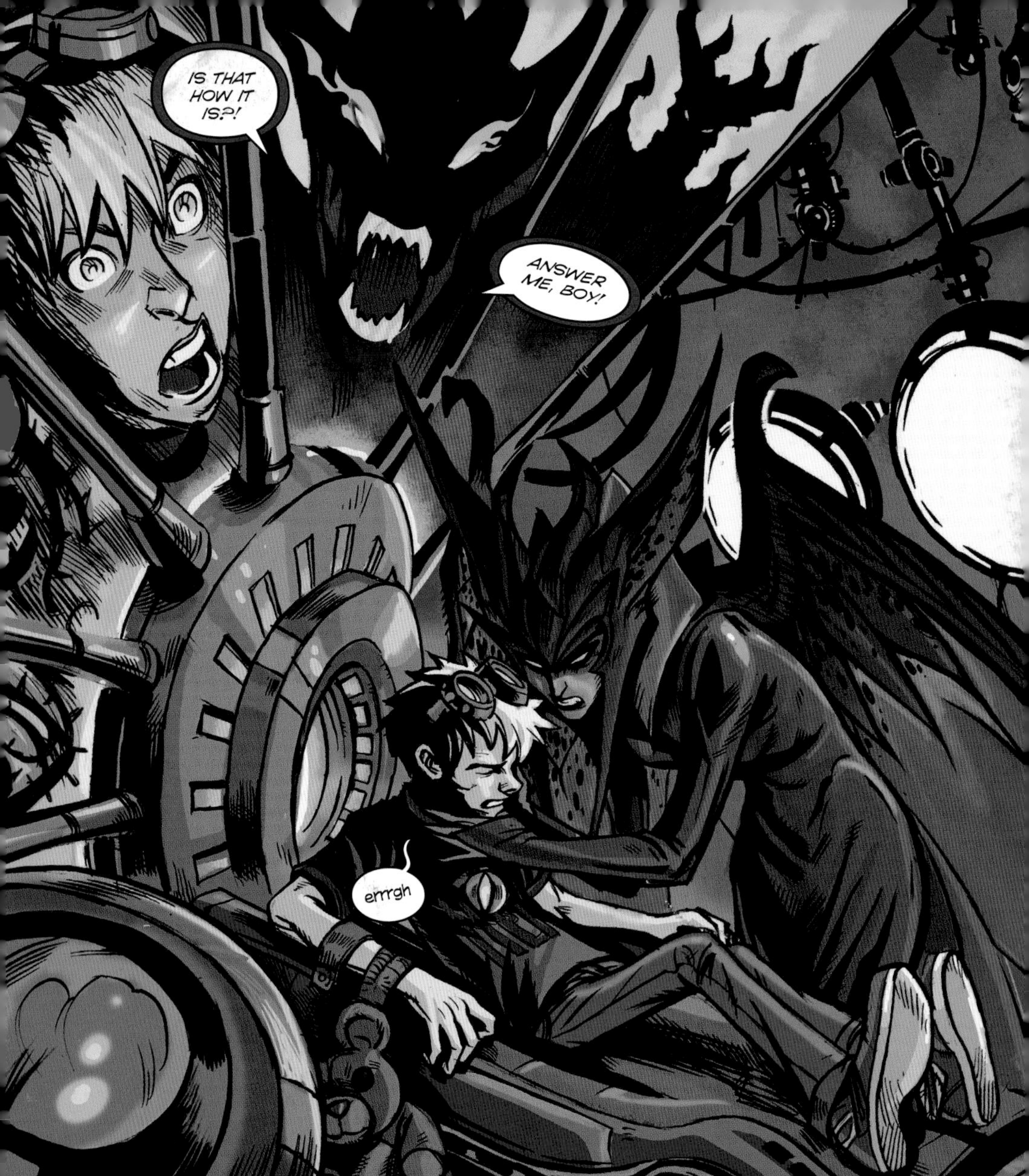
IS THAT HOW IT IS?!
ANSWER ME, BOY!
errrgh

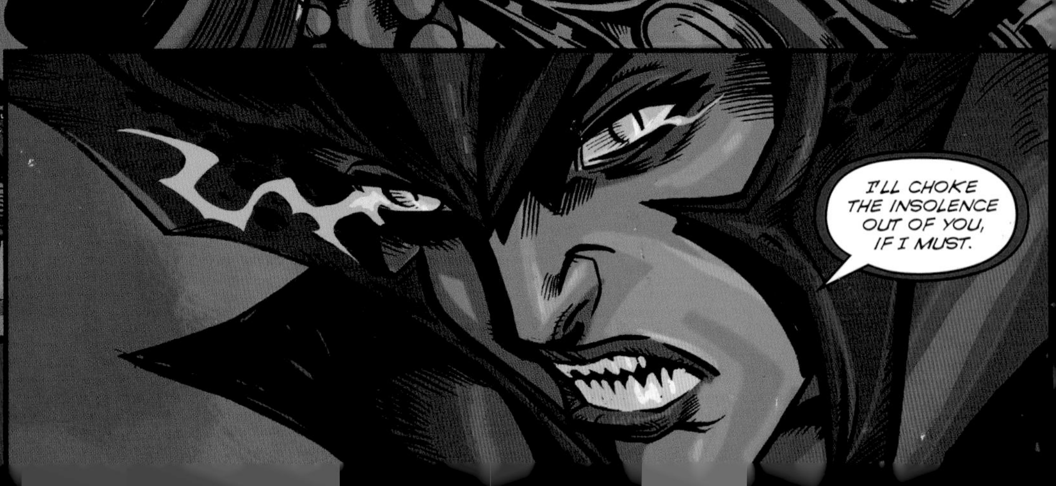
I'LL CHOKE THE INSOLENCE OUT OF YOU, IF I MUST.

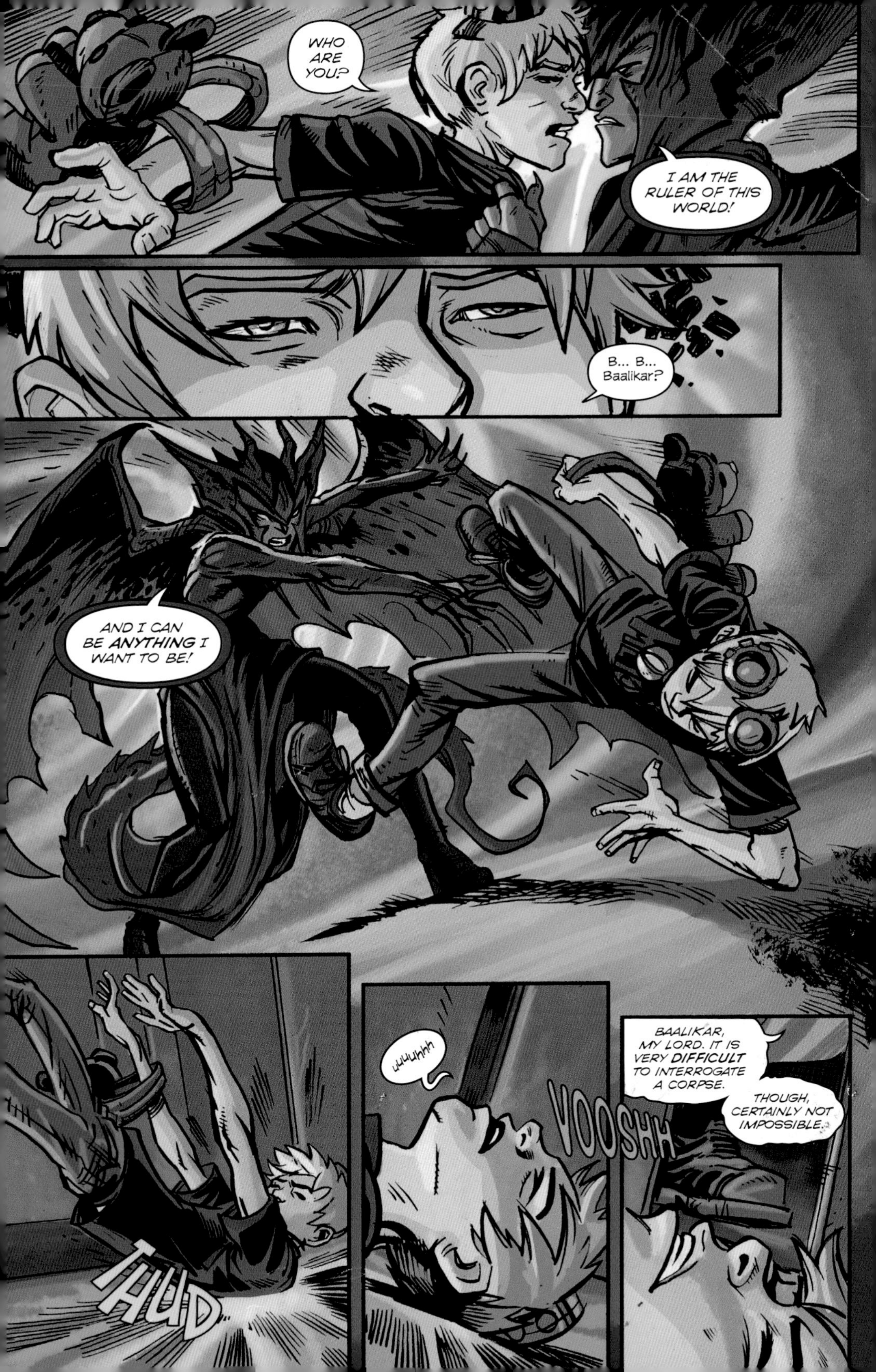
WHO ARE YOU?
I AM THE RULER OF THIS WORLD!
B... B... Baalikar?
AND I CAN BE ANYTHING I WANT TO BE!
THUD
uuuuhhh
VOOSHH
BAALIKAR, MY LORD. IT IS VERY DIFFICULT TO INTERROGATE A CORPSE.
THOUGH, CERTAINLY NOT IMPOSSIBLE.

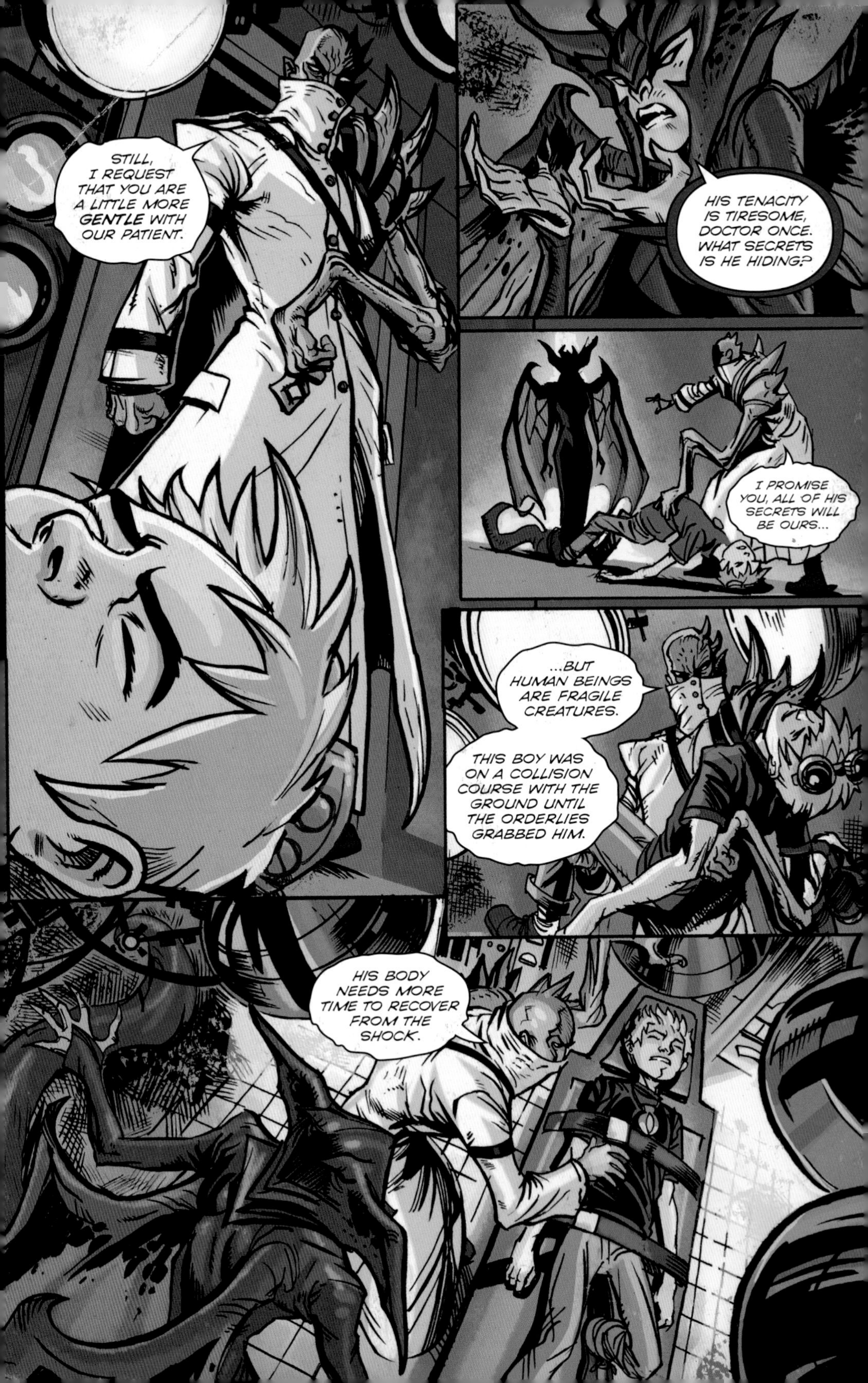
STILL, I REQUEST THAT YOU ARE A LITTLE MORE GENTLE WITH OUR PATIENT.
HIS TENACITY IS TIRESOME, DOCTOR ONCE. WHAT SECRETS IS HE HIDING?
I PROMISE YOU, ALL OF HIS SECRETS WILL BE OURS...
...BUT HUMAN BEINGS ARE FRAGILE CREATURES.
THIS BOY WAS ON A COLLISION COURSE WITH THE GROUND UNTIL THE ORDERLIES GRABBED HIM.
HIS BODY NEEDS MORE TIME TO RECOVER FROM THE SHOCK.

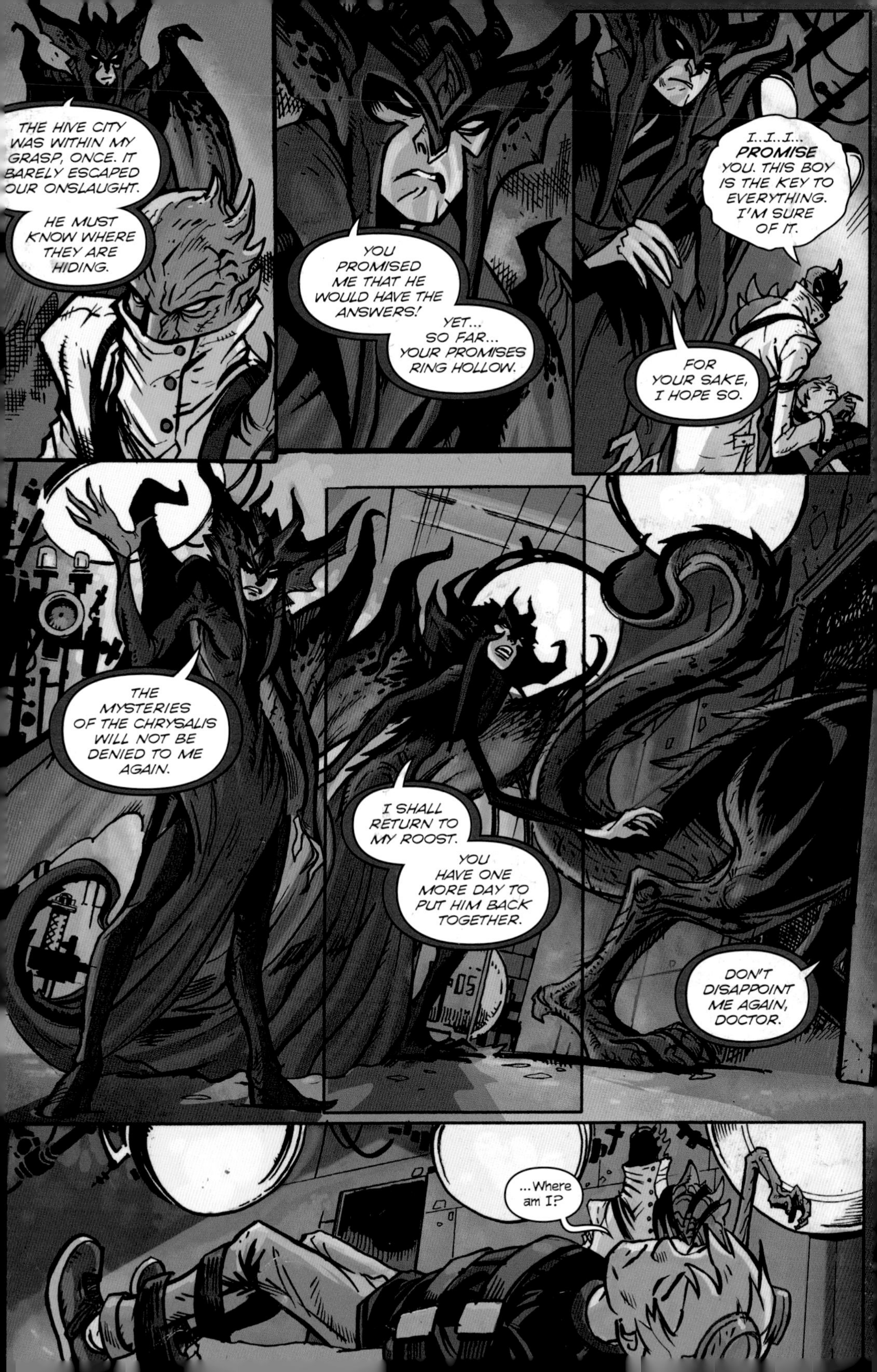
THE HIVE CITY WAS WITHIN MY GRASP, ONCE. IT BARELY ESCAPED OUR ONSLAUGHT.
HE MUST KNOW WHERE THEY ARE HIDING.
YOU PROMISED ME THAT HE WOULD HAVE THE ANSWERS!
YET... SO FAR... YOUR PROMISES RING HOLLOW.
I...I...I... PROMISE YOU. THIS BOY IS THE KEY TO EVERYTHING. I'M SURE OF IT.
FOR YOUR SAKE, I HOPE SO.
THE MYSTERIES OF THE CHRYSALIS WILL NOT BE DENIED TO ME AGAIN.
I SHALL RETURN TO MY ROOST.
YOU HAVE ONE MORE DAY TO PUT HIM BACK TOGETHER.
DON'T DISAPPOINT ME AGAIN, DOCTOR.
...Where am I?

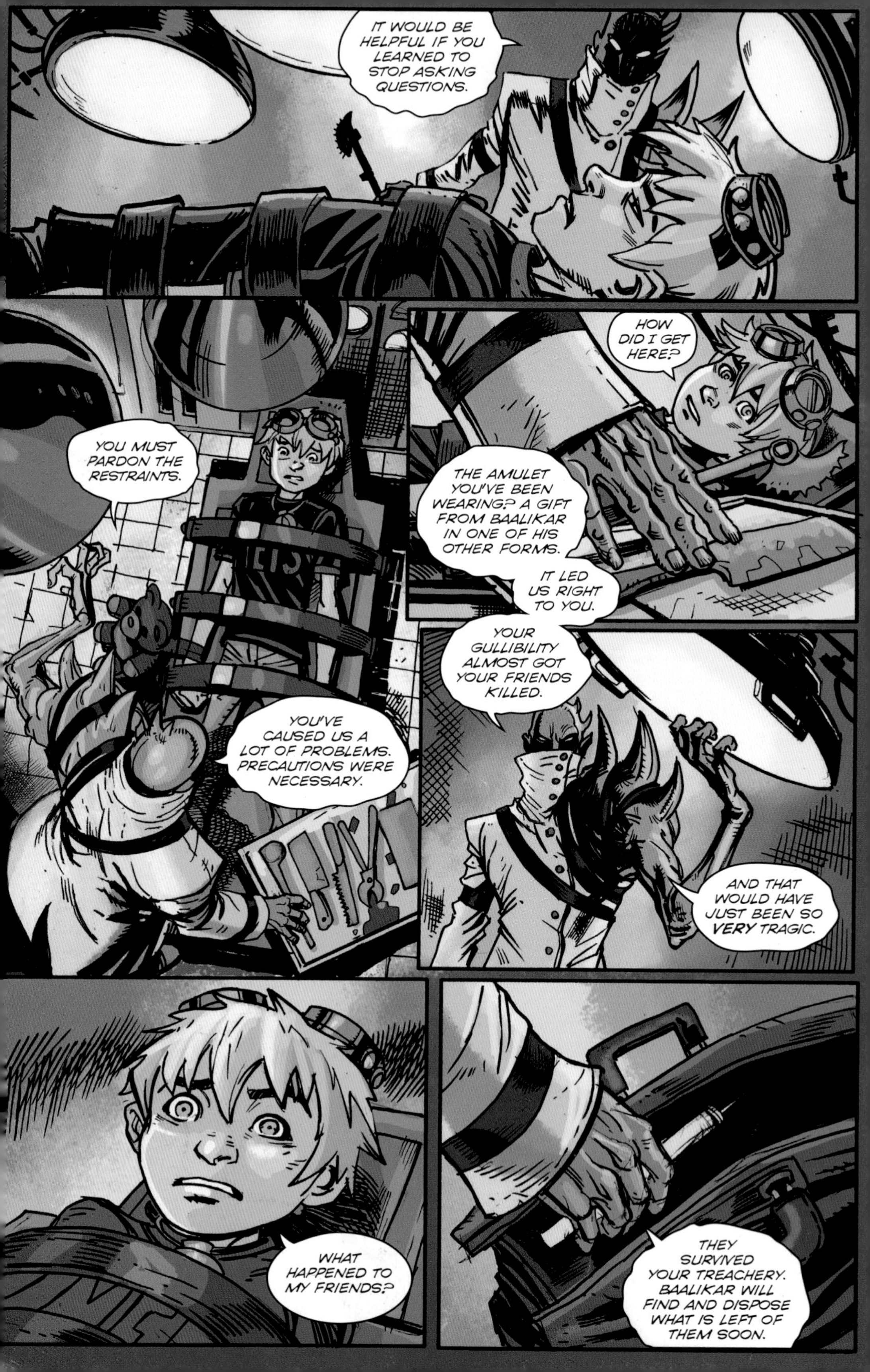
IT WOULD BE HELPFUL IF YOU LEARNED TO STOP ASKING QUESTIONS.
YOU MUST PARDON THE RESTRAINTS.
YOU'VE CAUSED US A LOT OF PROBLEMS. PRECAUTIONS WERE NECESSARY.
HOW DID I GET HERE?
THE AMULET YOU'VE BEEN WEARING? A GIFT FROM BAALIKAR IN ONE OF HIS OTHER FORMS.
IT LED US RIGHT TO YOU.
YOUR GULLIBILITY ALMOST GOT YOUR FRIENDS KILLED.
AND THAT WOULD HAVE JUST BEEN SO VERY TRAGIC.
WHAT HAPPENED TO MY FRIENDS?
THEY SURVIVED YOUR TREACHERY. BAALIKAR WILL FIND AND DISPOSE WHAT IS LEFT OF THEM SOON.

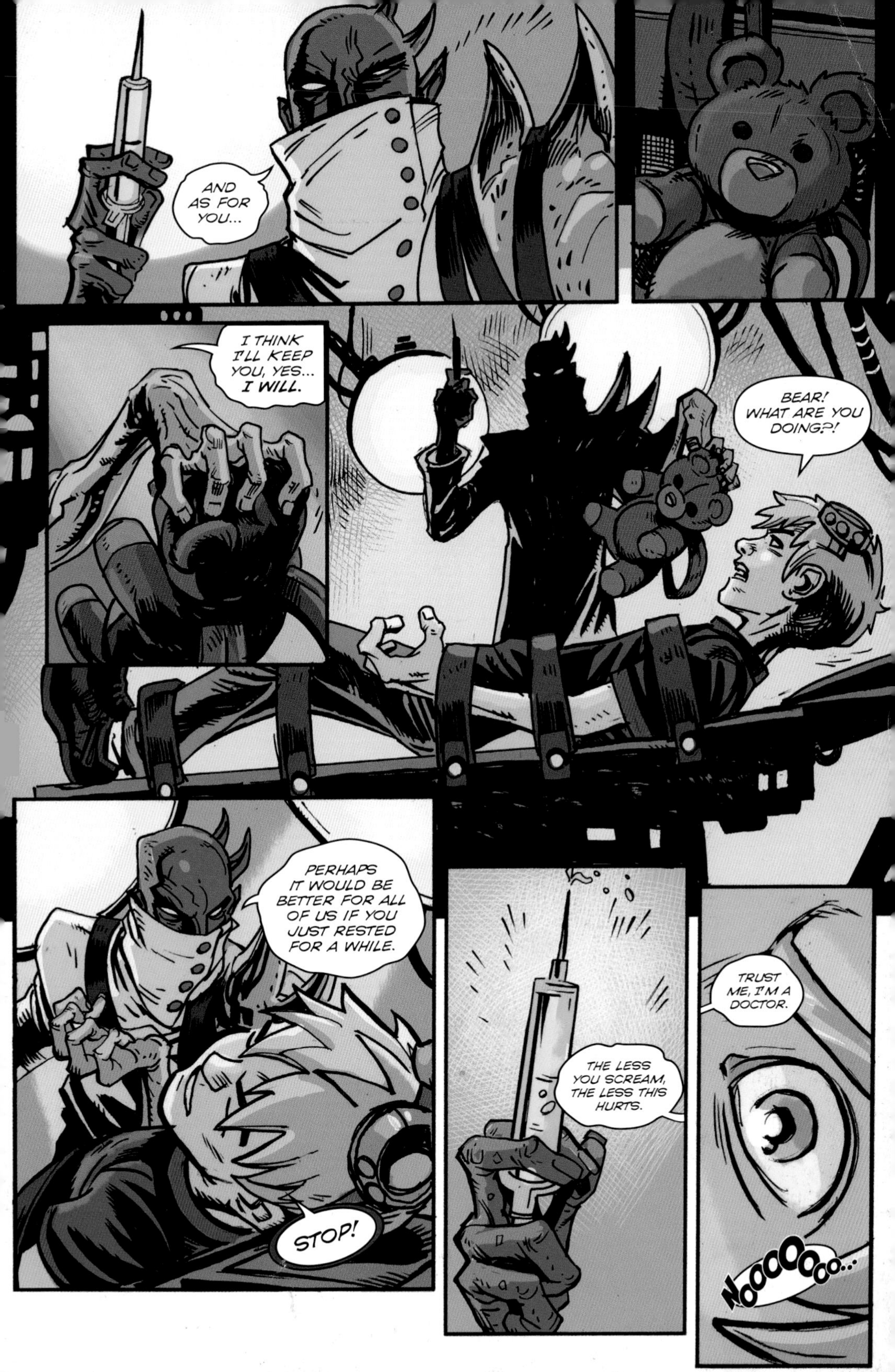
AND AS FOR YOU...
I THINK I'LL KEEP YOU, YES... I WILL.
BEAR! WHAT ARE YOU DOING?!
PERHAPS IT WOULD BE BETTER FOR ALL OF US IF YOU JUST RESTED FOR A WHILE.
STOP!
THE LESS YOU SCREAM, THE LESS THIS HURTS.
TRUST ME, I'M A DOCTOR.
NOOOOOOO...

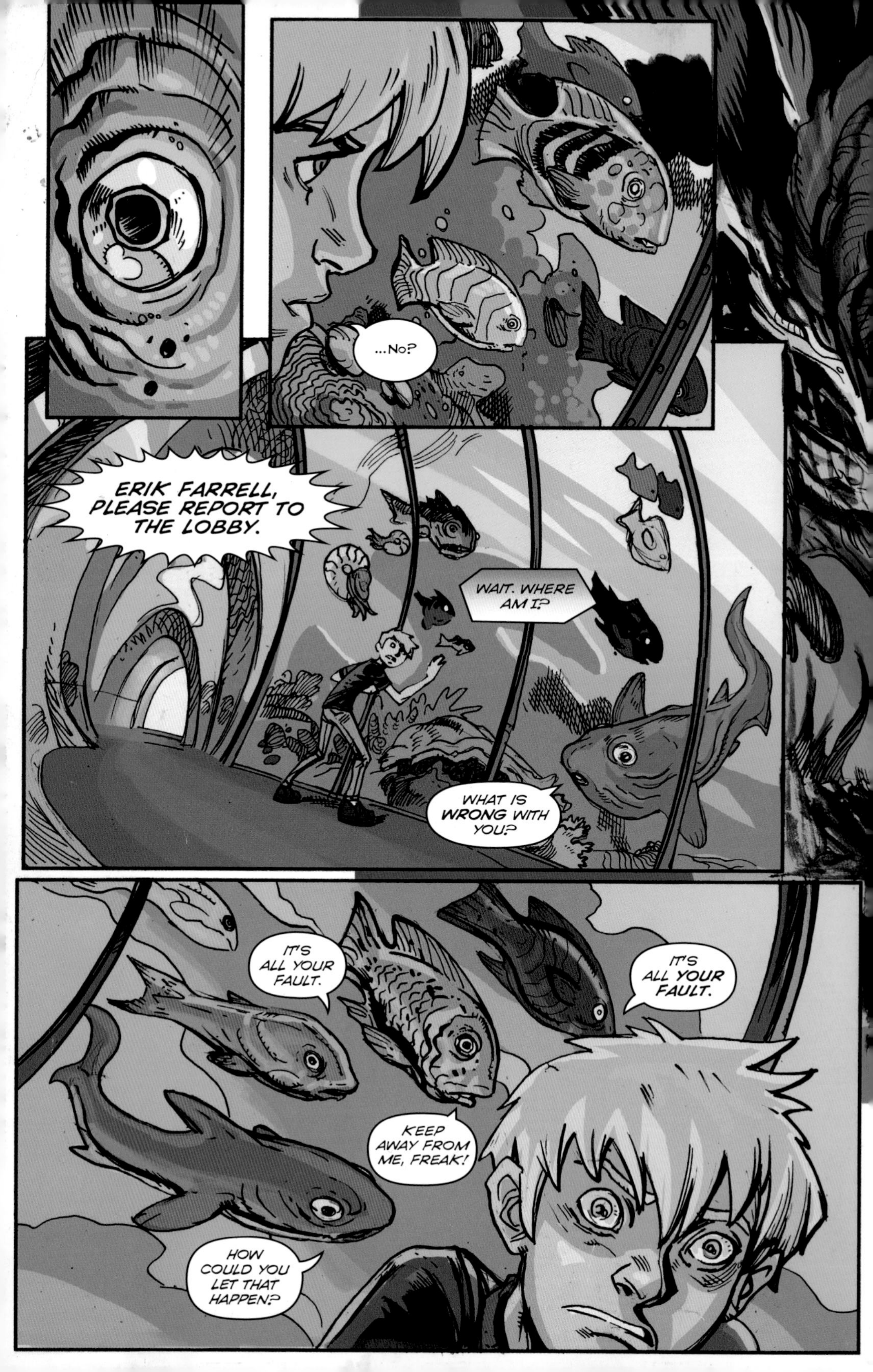
...No?
ERIK FARRELL, PLEASE REPORT TO THE LOBBY.
WAIT. WHERE AM I?
WHAT IS WRONG WITH YOU?
IT'S ALL YOUR FAULT.
IT'S ALL YOUR FAULT.
KEEP AWAY FROM ME, FREAK!
HOW COULD YOU LET THAT HAPPEN?

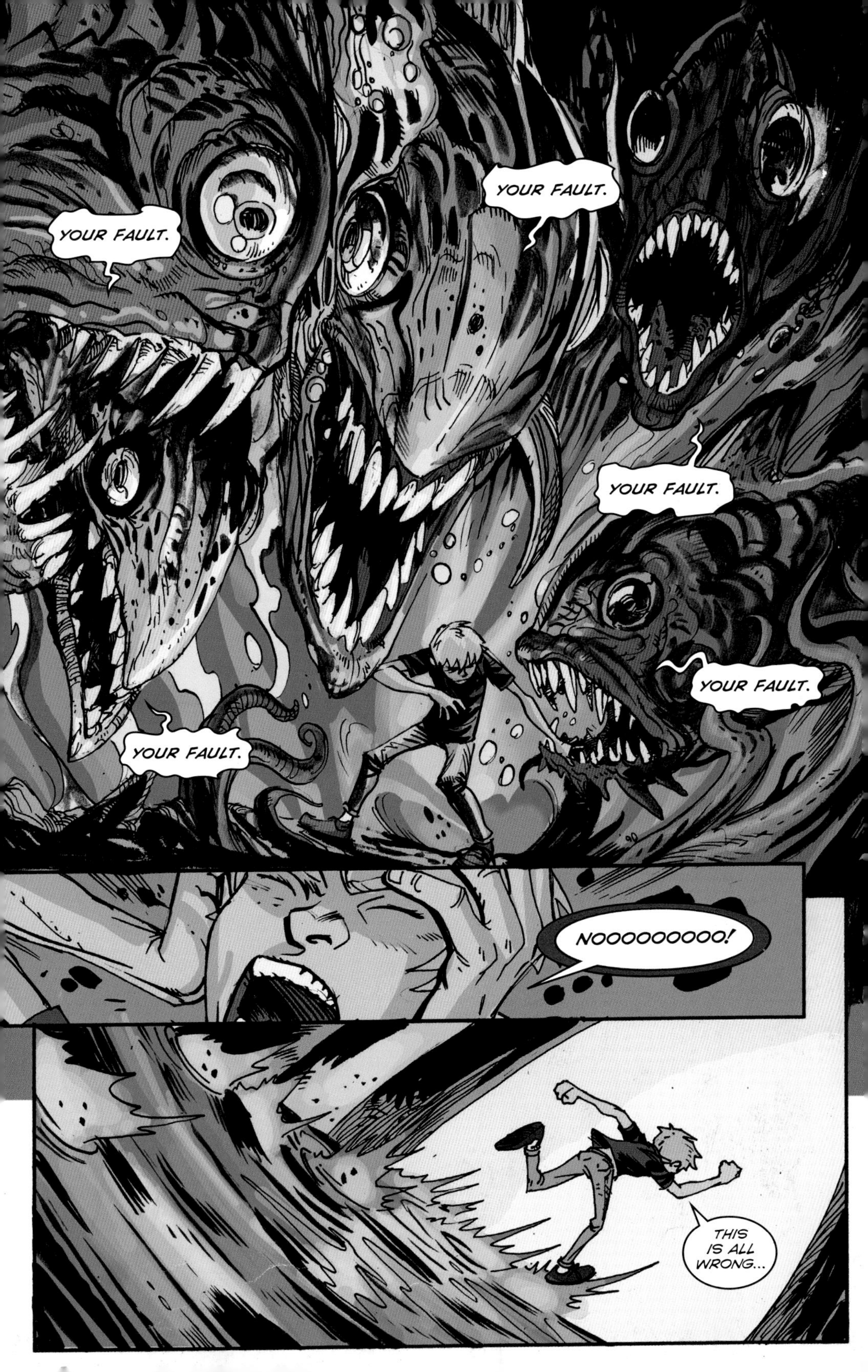
YOUR FAULT.
YOUR FAULT.
YOUR FAULT.
YOUR FAULT.
YOUR FAULT.
NOOOOOOOOO!
THIS IS ALL WRONG...

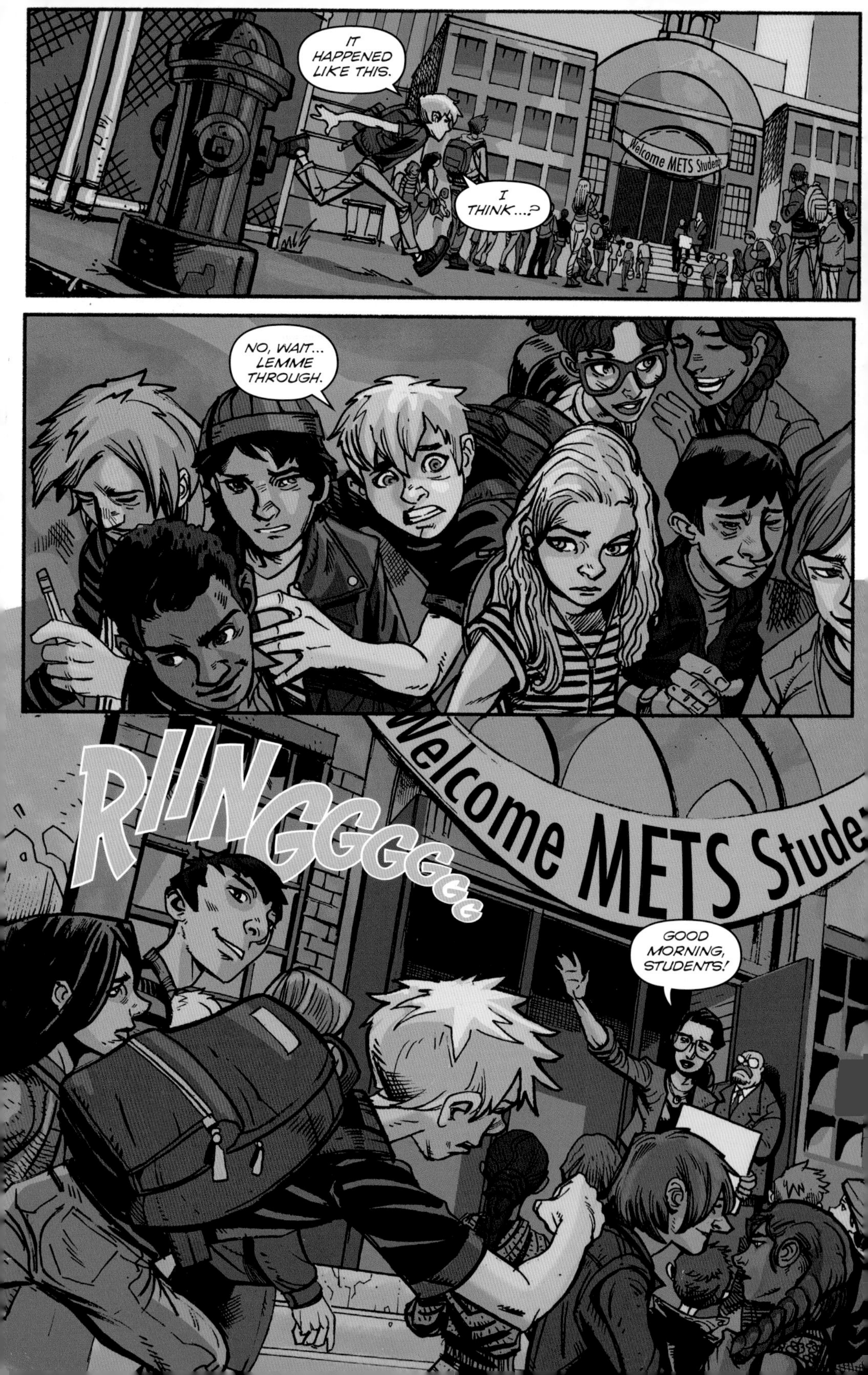
IT HAPPENED LIKE THIS.
I THINK...?
Welcome METS Students
NO, WAIT... LEMME THROUGH.
RIINGGGGG
Welcome METS Stude
GOOD MORNING, STUDENTS!

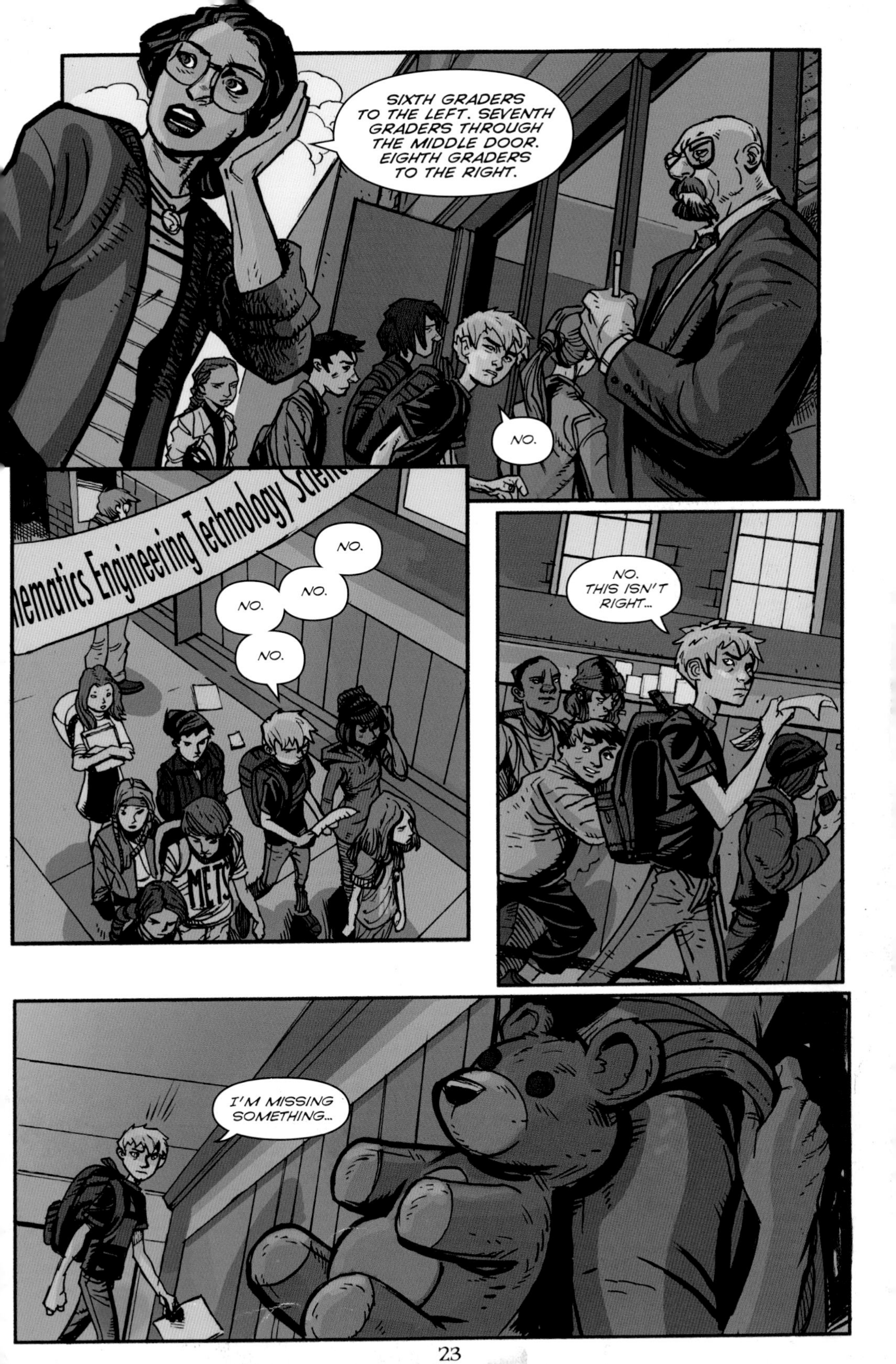
SIXTH GRADERS TO THE LEFT. SEVENTH GRADERS THROUGH THE MIDDLE DOOR. EIGHTH GRADERS TO THE RIGHT.
NO.
nematics Engineering Technology Scien
NO.
NO.
NO.
NO.
NO. THIS ISN'T RIGHT...
I'M MISSING SOMETHING...

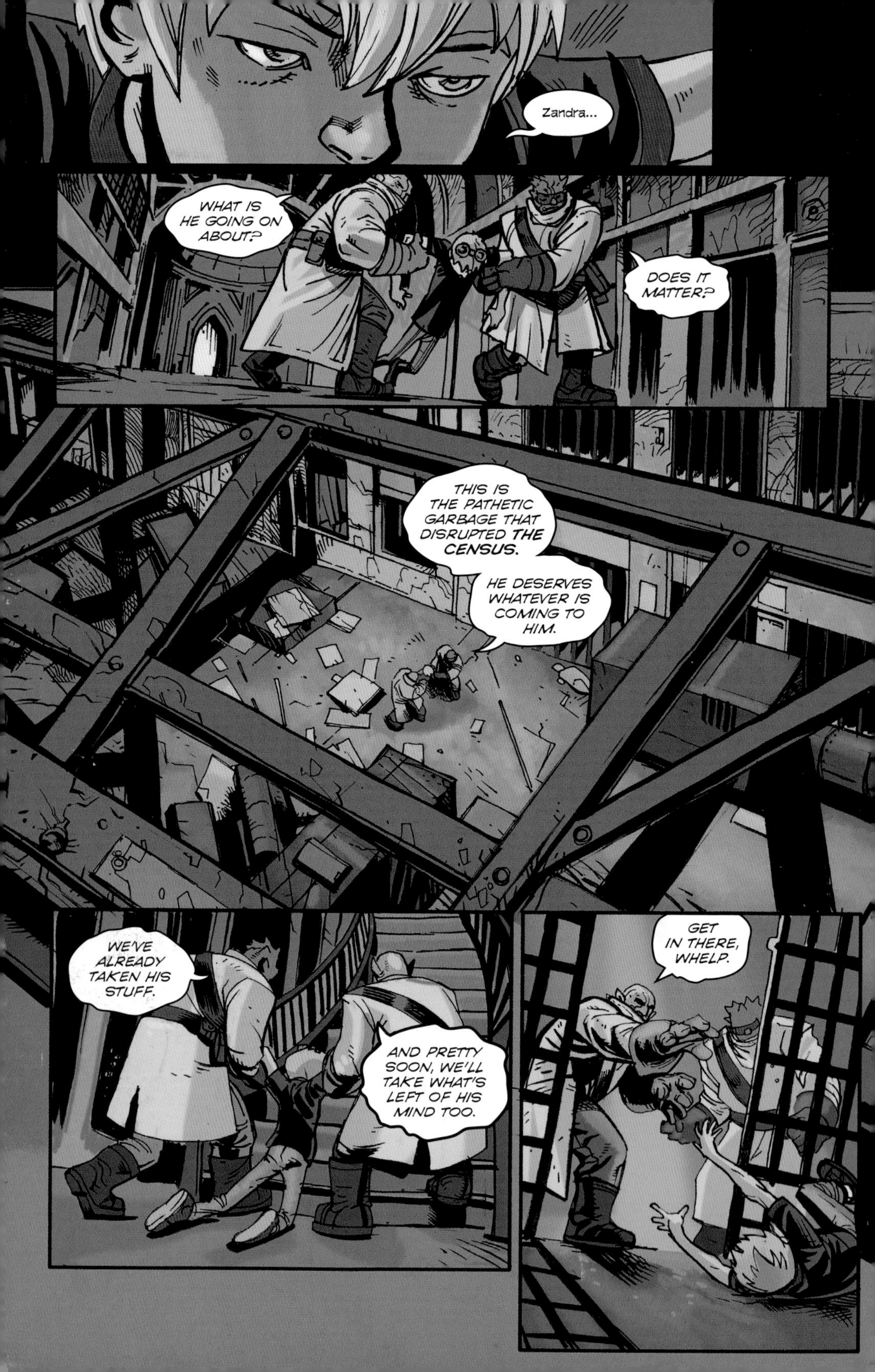
Zandra...
WHAT IS HE GOING ON ABOUT?
DOES IT MATTER?
THIS IS THE PATHETIC GARBAGE THAT DISRUPTED **THE CENSUS.**
HE DESERVES WHATEVER IS COMING TO HIM.
WE'VE ALREADY TAKEN HIS STUFF.
AND PRETTY SOON, WE'LL TAKE WHAT'S LEFT OF HIS MIND TOO.
GET IN THERE, WHELP.

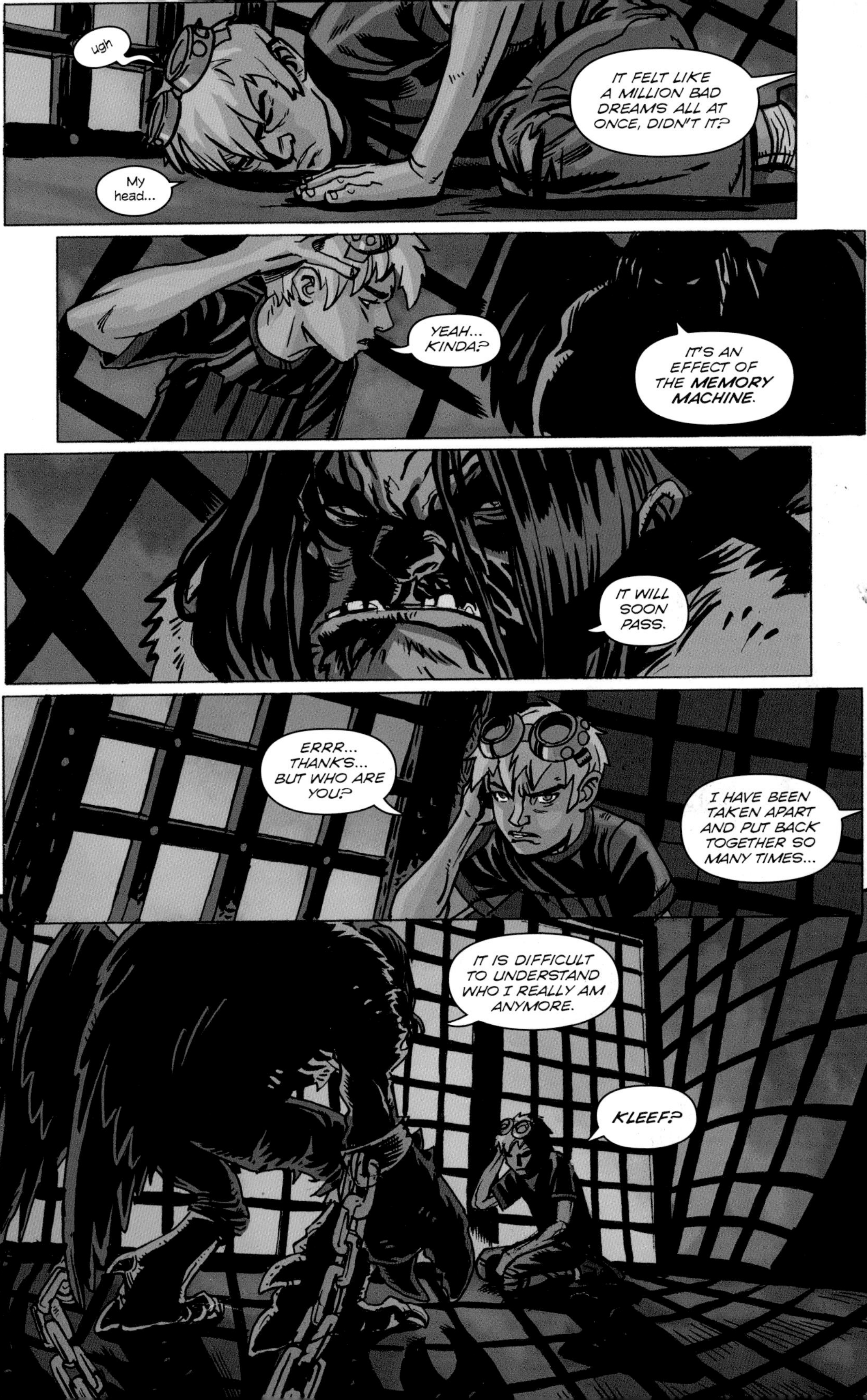
ugh
My head...
IT FELT LIKE A MILLION BAD DREAMS ALL AT ONCE, DIDN'T IT?
YEAH... KINDA?
IT'S AN EFFECT OF THE MEMORY MACHINE.
IT WILL SOON PASS.
ERRR... THANKS... BUT WHO ARE YOU?
I HAVE BEEN TAKEN APART AND PUT BACK TOGETHER SO MANY TIMES...
IT IS DIFFICULT TO UNDERSTAND WHO I REALLY AM ANYMORE.
KLEEF?

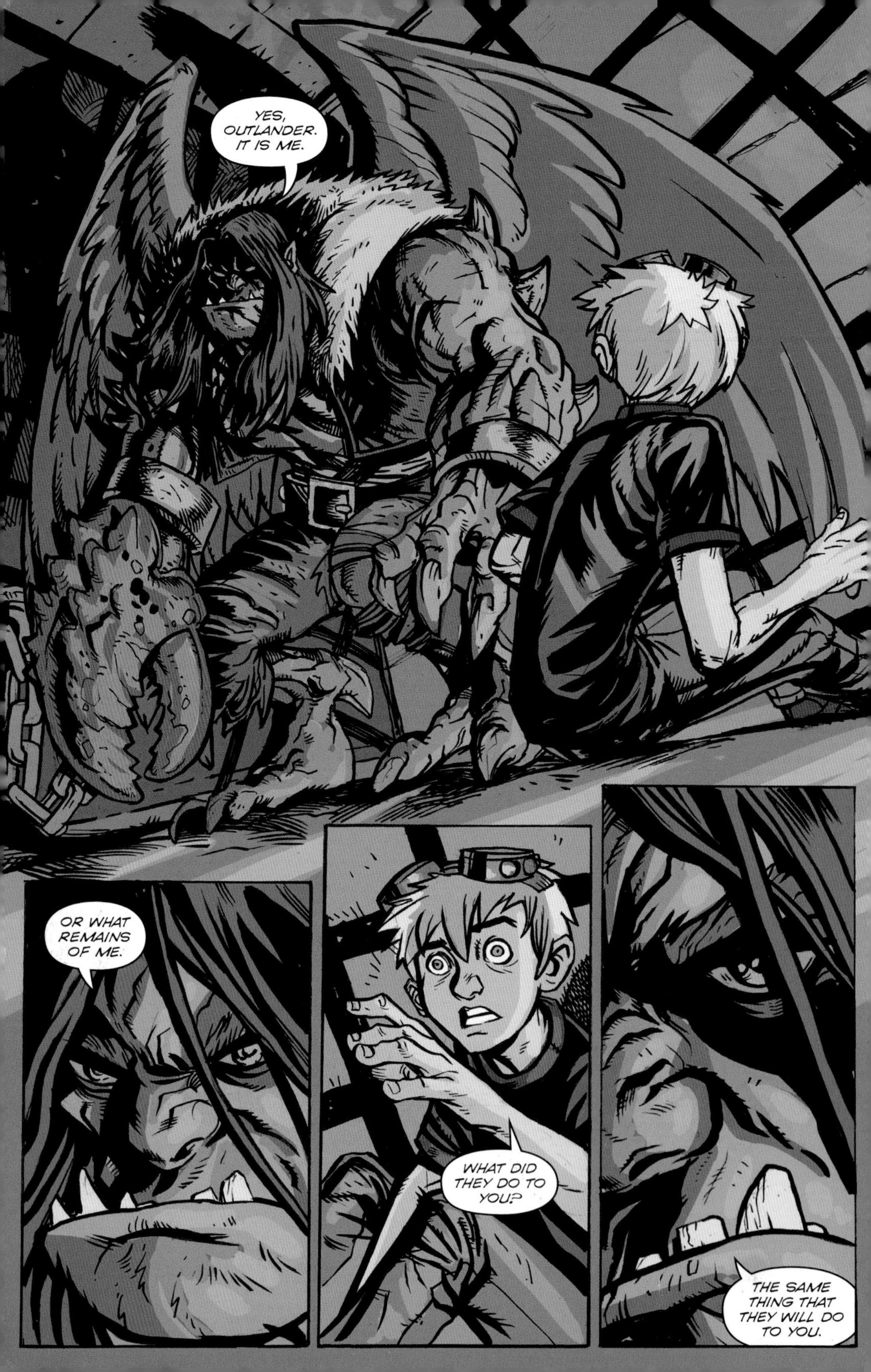

YES, OUTLANDER. IT IS ME.
OR WHAT REMAINS OF ME.
WHAT DID THEY DO TO YOU?
THE SAME THING THAT THEY WILL DO TO YOU.

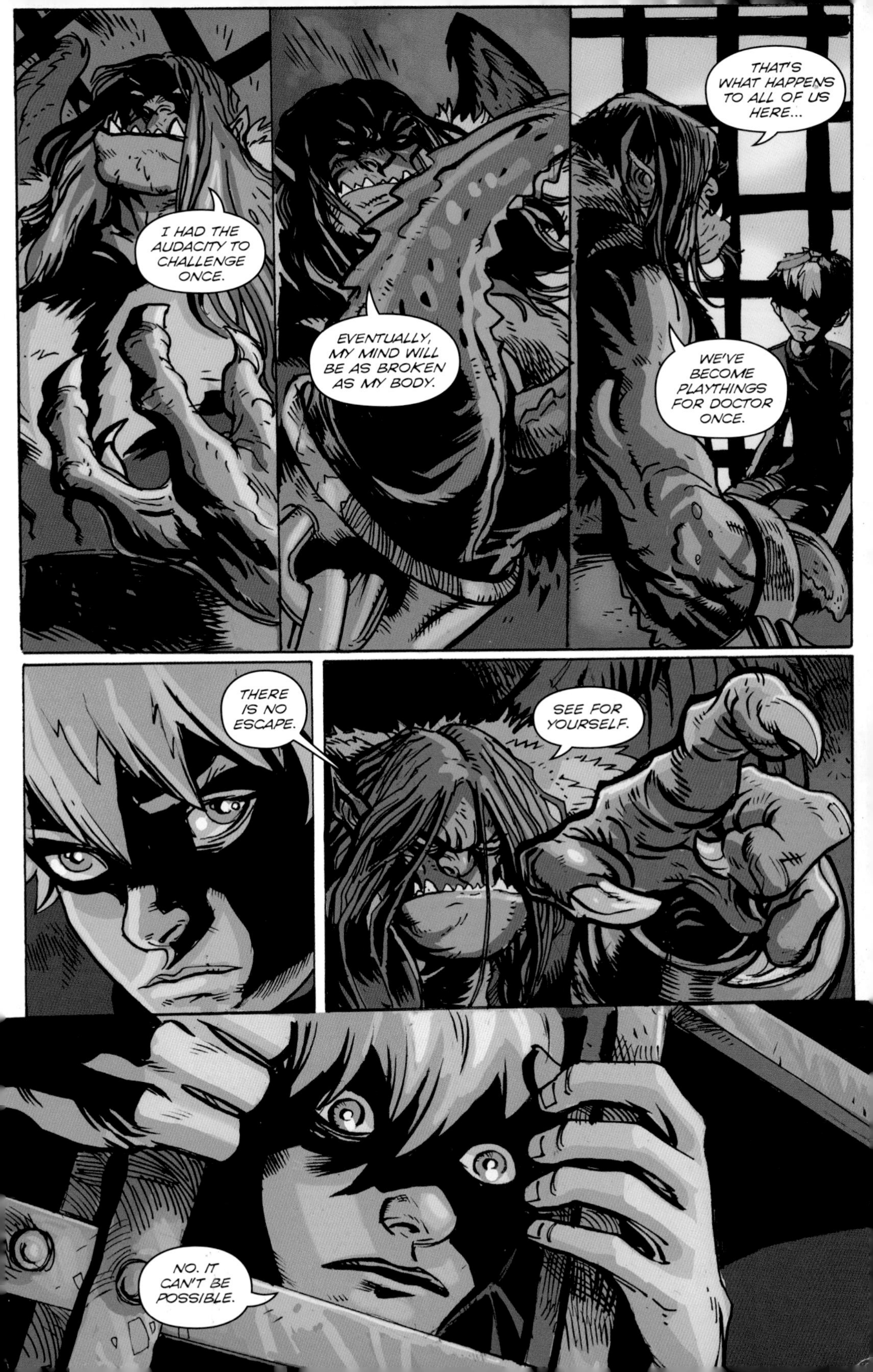
I HAD THE AUDACITY TO CHALLENGE ONCE.
EVENTUALLY, MY MIND WILL BE AS BROKEN AS MY BODY.
THAT'S WHAT HAPPENS TO ALL OF US HERE...
WE'VE BECOME PLAYTHINGS FOR DOCTOR ONCE.
THERE IS NO ESCAPE.
SEE FOR YOURSELF.
NO. IT CAN'T BE POSSIBLE.

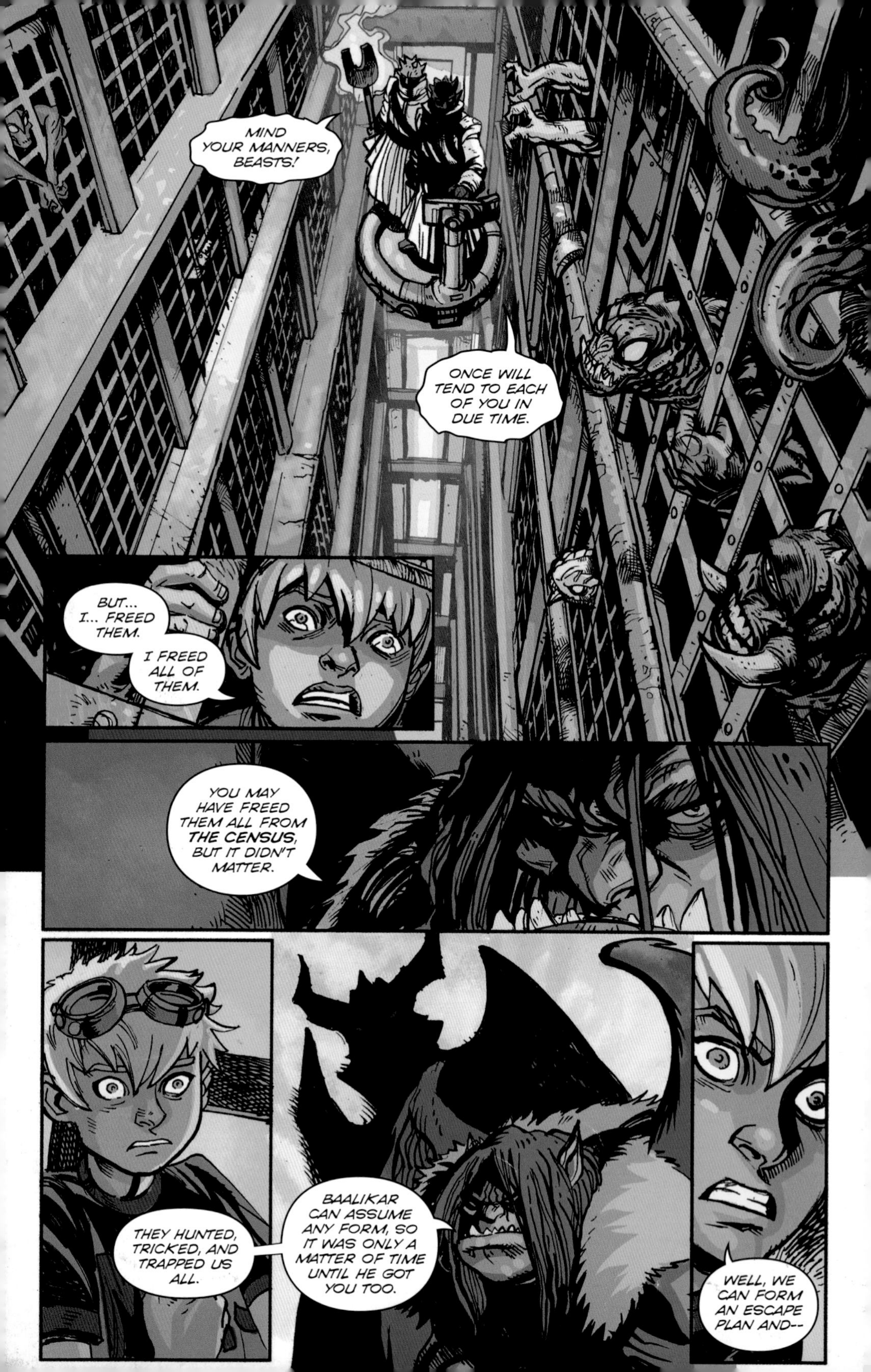
MIND YOUR MANNERS, BEASTS!
ONCE WILL TEND TO EACH OF YOU IN DUE TIME.
BUT... I... FREED THEM.
I FREED ALL OF THEM.
YOU MAY HAVE FREED THEM ALL FROM THE CENSUS, BUT IT DIDN'T MATTER.
THEY HUNTED, TRICKED, AND TRAPPED US ALL.
BAALIKAR CAN ASSUME ANY FORM, SO IT WAS ONLY A MATTER OF TIME UNTIL HE GOT YOU TOO.
WELL, WE CAN FORM AN ESCAPE PLAN AND--

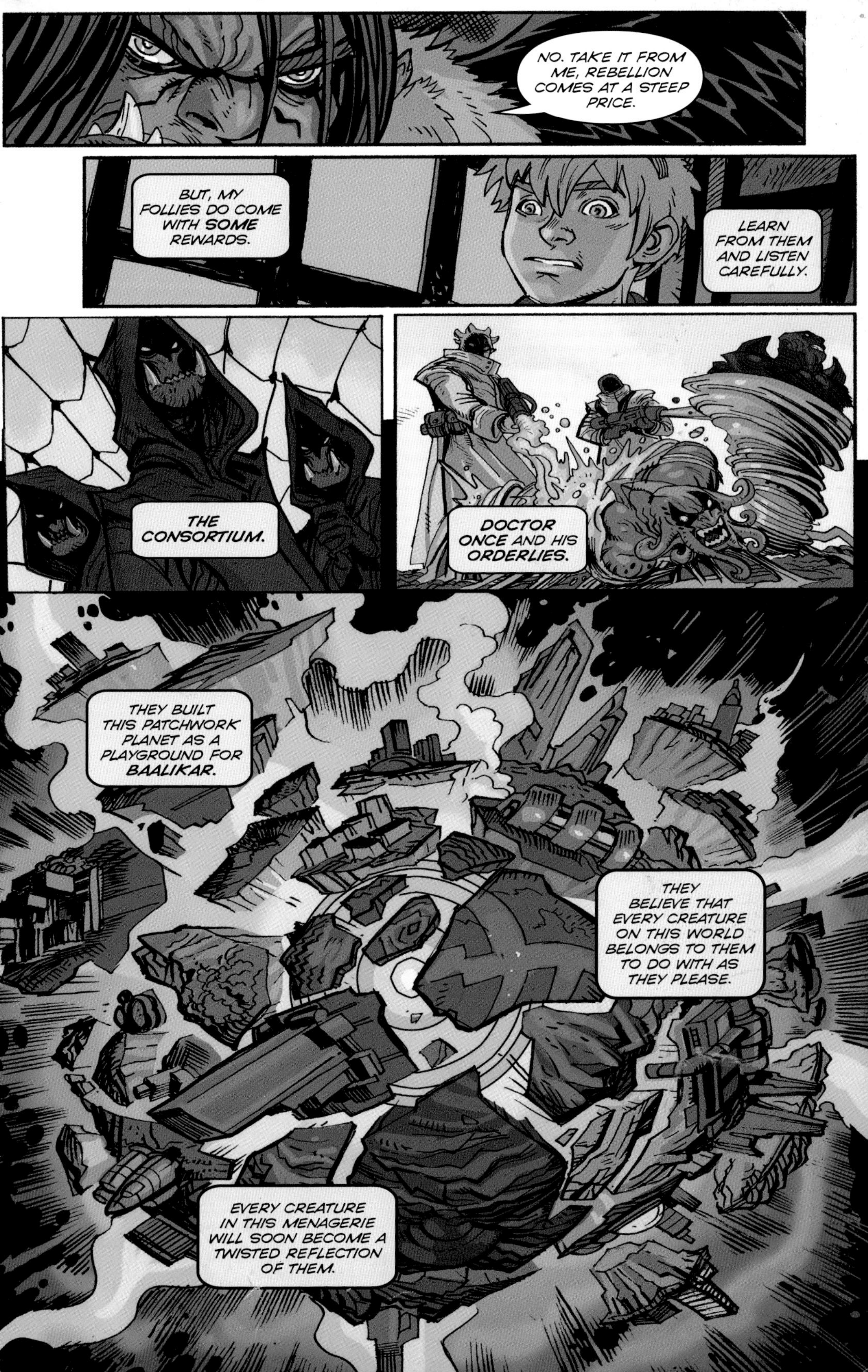
NO. TAKE IT FROM ME, REBELLION COMES AT A STEEP PRICE.
BUT, MY FOLLIES DO COME WITH SOME REWARDS.
LEARN FROM THEM AND LISTEN CAREFULLY.
THE CONSORTIUM.
DOCTOR ONCE AND HIS ORDERLIES.
THEY BUILT THIS PATCHWORK PLANET AS A PLAYGROUND FOR BAALIKAR.
THEY BELIEVE THAT EVERY CREATURE ON THIS WORLD BELONGS TO THEM TO DO WITH AS THEY PLEASE.
EVERY CREATURE IN THIS MENAGERIE WILL SOON BECOME A TWISTED REFLECTION OF THEM.

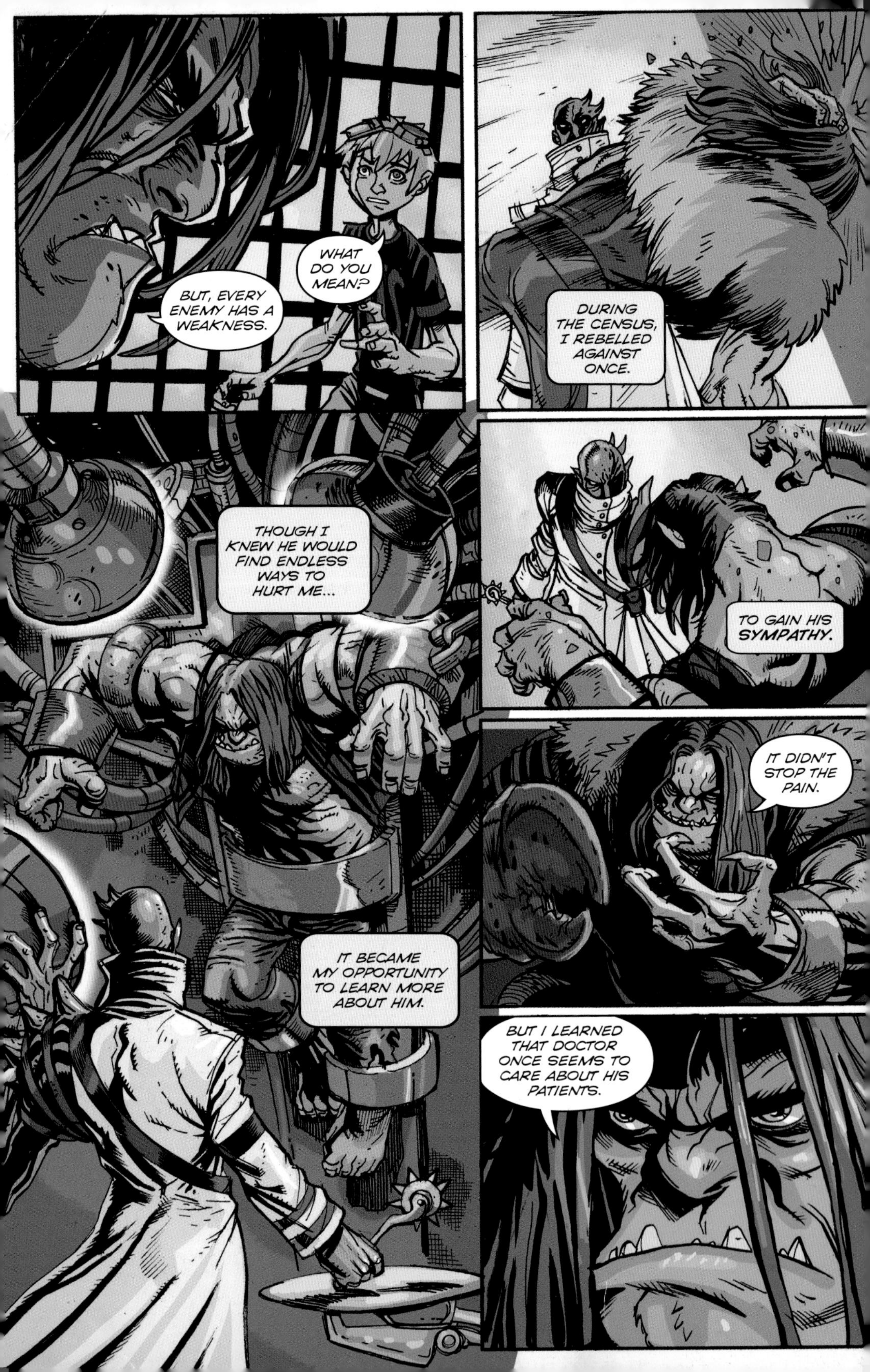
BUT, EVERY ENEMY HAS A WEAKNESS.
WHAT DO YOU MEAN?
DURING THE CENSUS, I REBELLED AGAINST ONCE.
THOUGH I KNEW HE WOULD FIND ENDLESS WAYS TO HURT ME...
IT BECAME MY OPPORTUNITY TO LEARN MORE ABOUT HIM.
TO GAIN HIS SYMPATHY.
IT DIDN'T STOP THE PAIN.
BUT I LEARNED THAT DOCTOR ONCE SEEMS TO CARE ABOUT HIS PATIENTS.

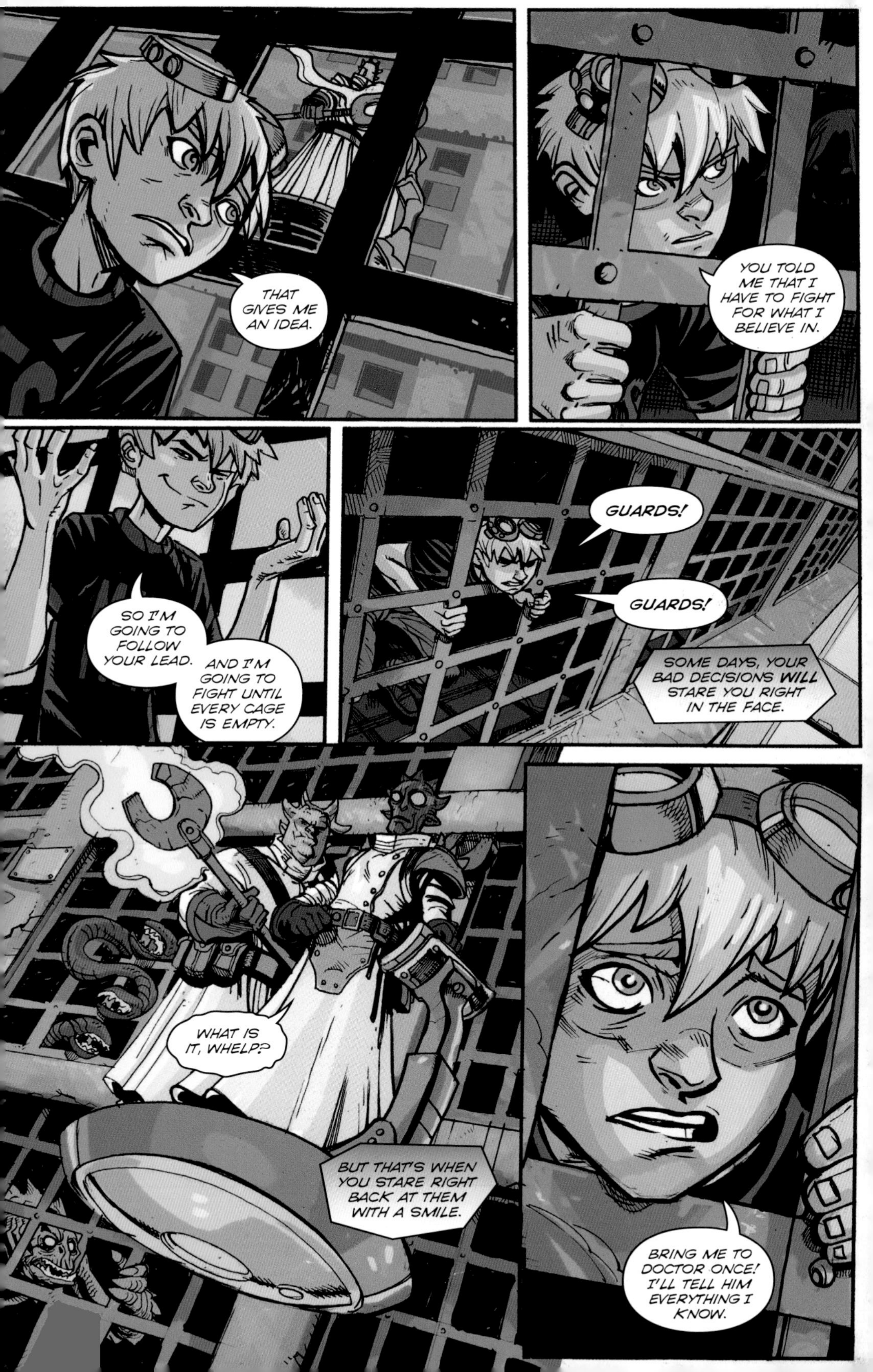
THAT GIVES ME AN IDEA.
YOU TOLD ME THAT I HAVE TO FIGHT FOR WHAT I BELIEVE IN.
SO I'M GOING TO FOLLOW YOUR LEAD.
AND I'M GOING TO FIGHT UNTIL EVERY CAGE IS EMPTY.
GUARDS!
GUARDS!
SOME DAYS, YOUR BAD DECISIONS WILL STARE YOU RIGHT IN THE FACE.
WHAT IS IT, WHELP?
BUT THAT'S WHEN YOU STARE RIGHT BACK AT THEM WITH A SMILE.
BRING ME TO DOCTOR ONCE! I'LL TELL HIM EVERYTHING I KNOW.

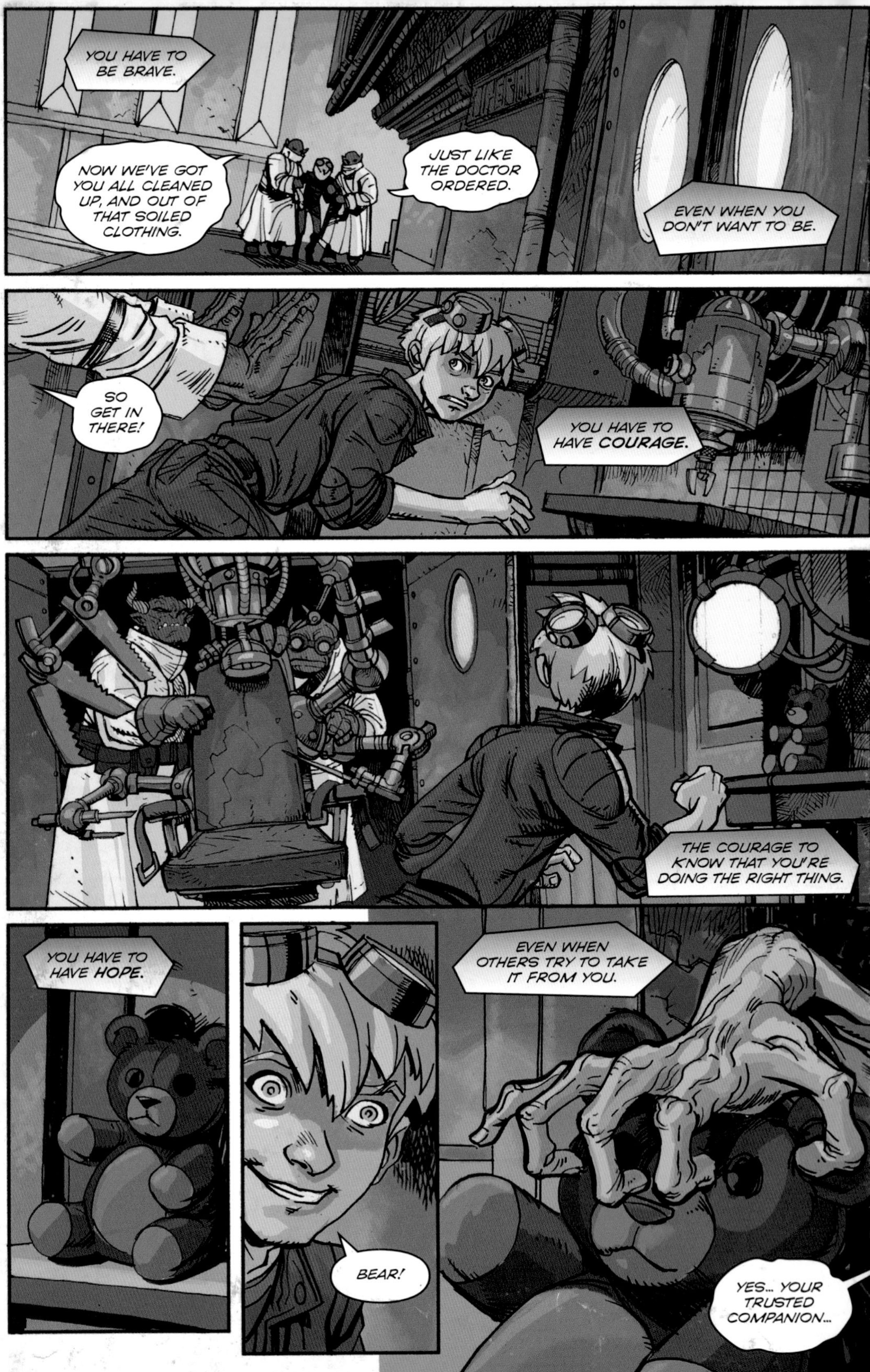
YOU HAVE TO BE BRAVE.
NOW WE'VE GOT YOU ALL CLEANED UP, AND OUT OF THAT SOILED CLOTHING.
JUST LIKE THE DOCTOR ORDERED.
EVEN WHEN YOU DON'T WANT TO BE.
SO GET IN THERE!
YOU HAVE TO HAVE COURAGE.
THE COURAGE TO KNOW THAT YOU'RE DOING THE RIGHT THING.
YOU HAVE TO HAVE HOPE.
EVEN WHEN OTHERS TRY TO TAKE IT FROM YOU.
BEAR!
YES... YOUR TRUSTED COMPANION...

AND NOW, MY LITTLE... HOSTAGE...

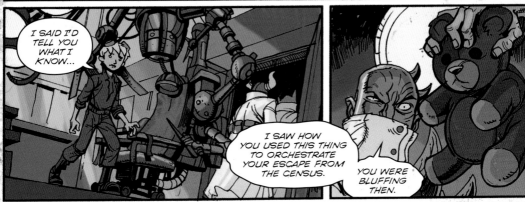

I SAID I'D TELL YOU WHAT I KNOW...

I SAW HOW YOU USED THIS THING TO ORCHESTRATE YOUR ESCAPE FROM THE CENSUS.

YOU WERE BLUFFING THEN.

YOU ARE BLUFFING NOW.

Leave Bear alone.

WHAT SORT OF GAME ARE YOU PLAYING, BOY?

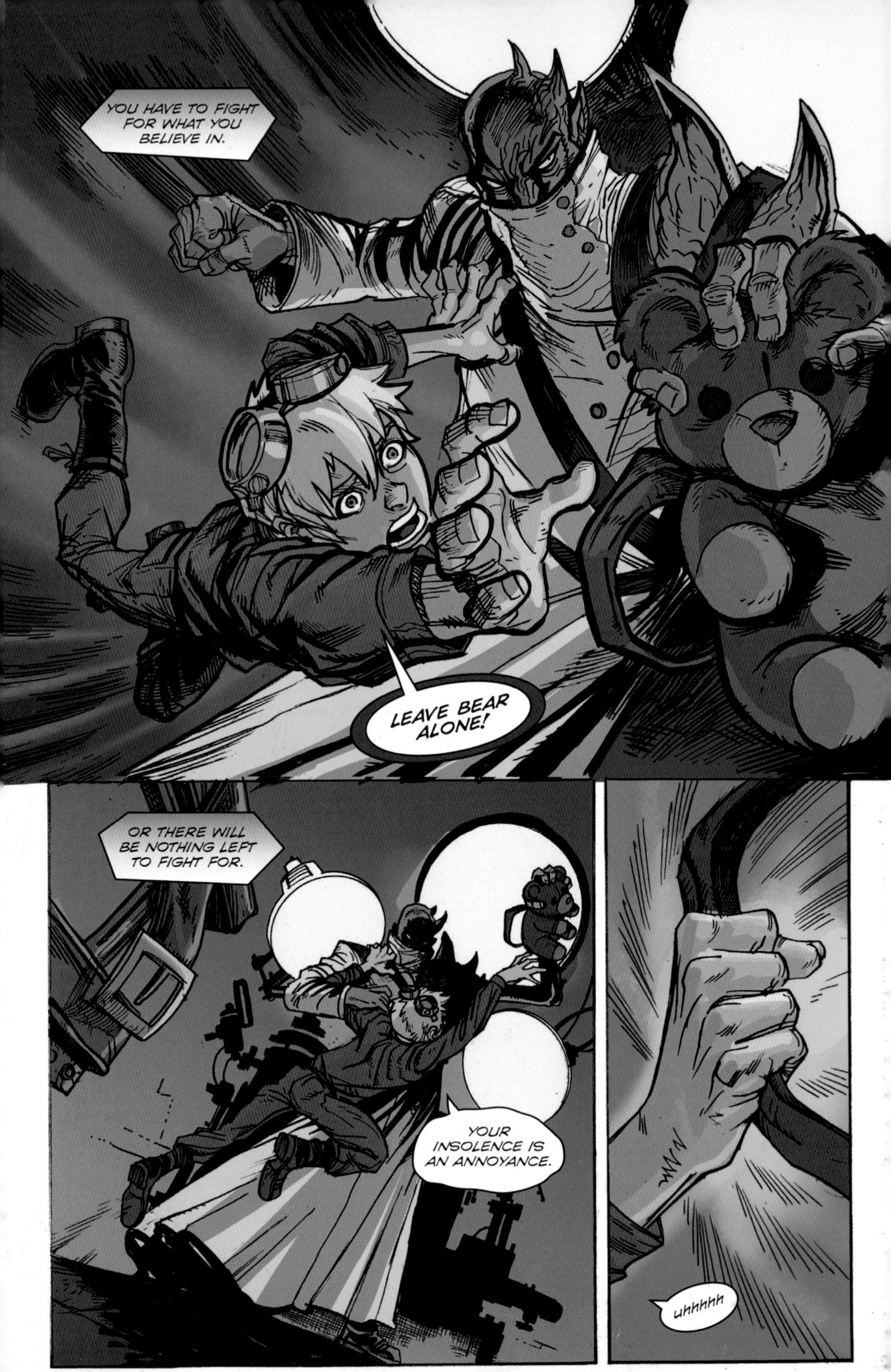
YOU HAVE TO FIGHT FOR WHAT YOU BELIEVE IN.
LEAVE BEAR ALONE!
OR THERE WILL BE NOTHING LEFT TO FIGHT FOR.
YOUR INSOLENCE IS AN ANNOYANCE.
uhhhhh

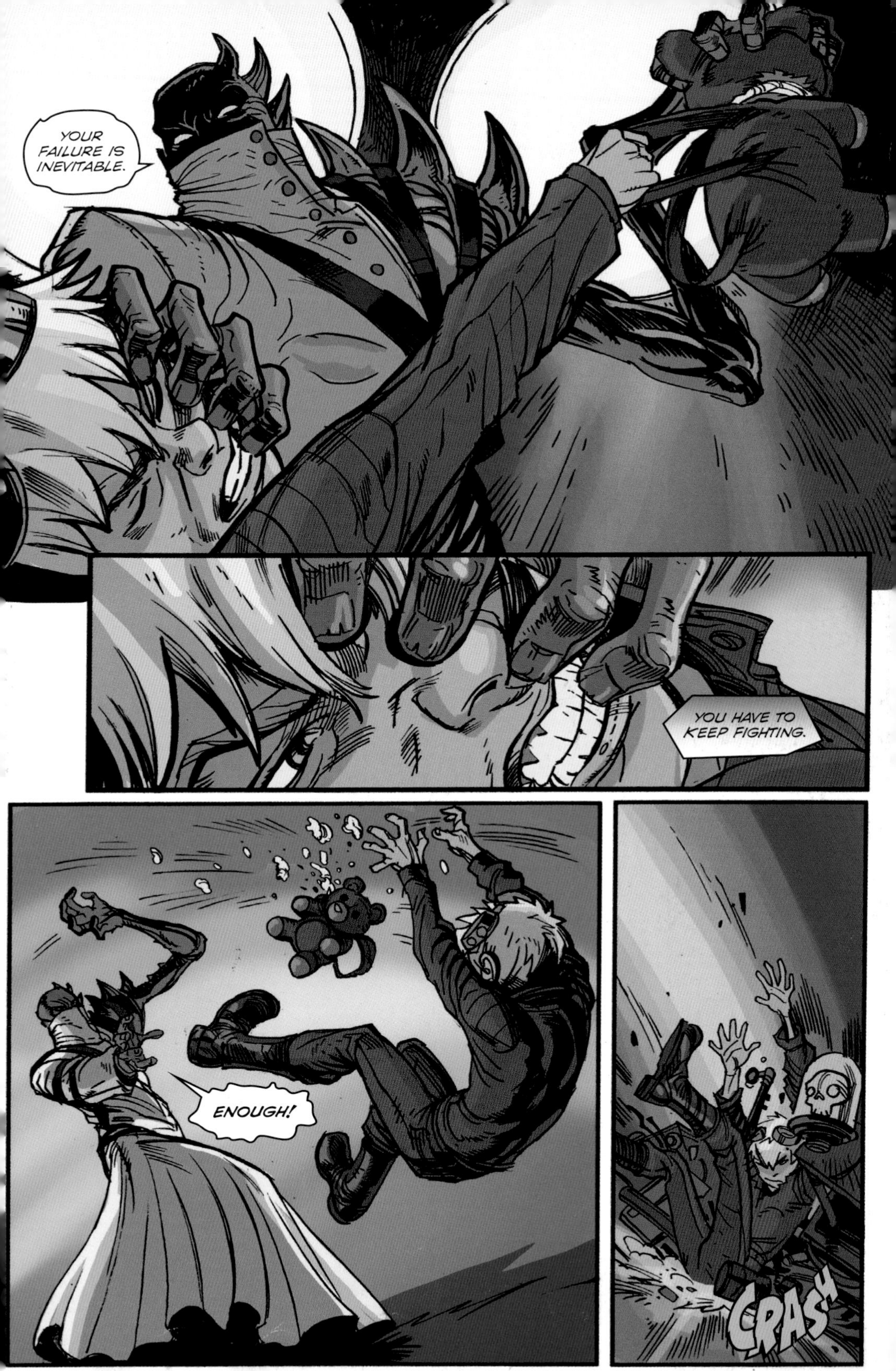
YOUR FAILURE IS INEVITABLE.
YOU HAVE TO KEEP FIGHTING.
ENOUGH!
CRASH

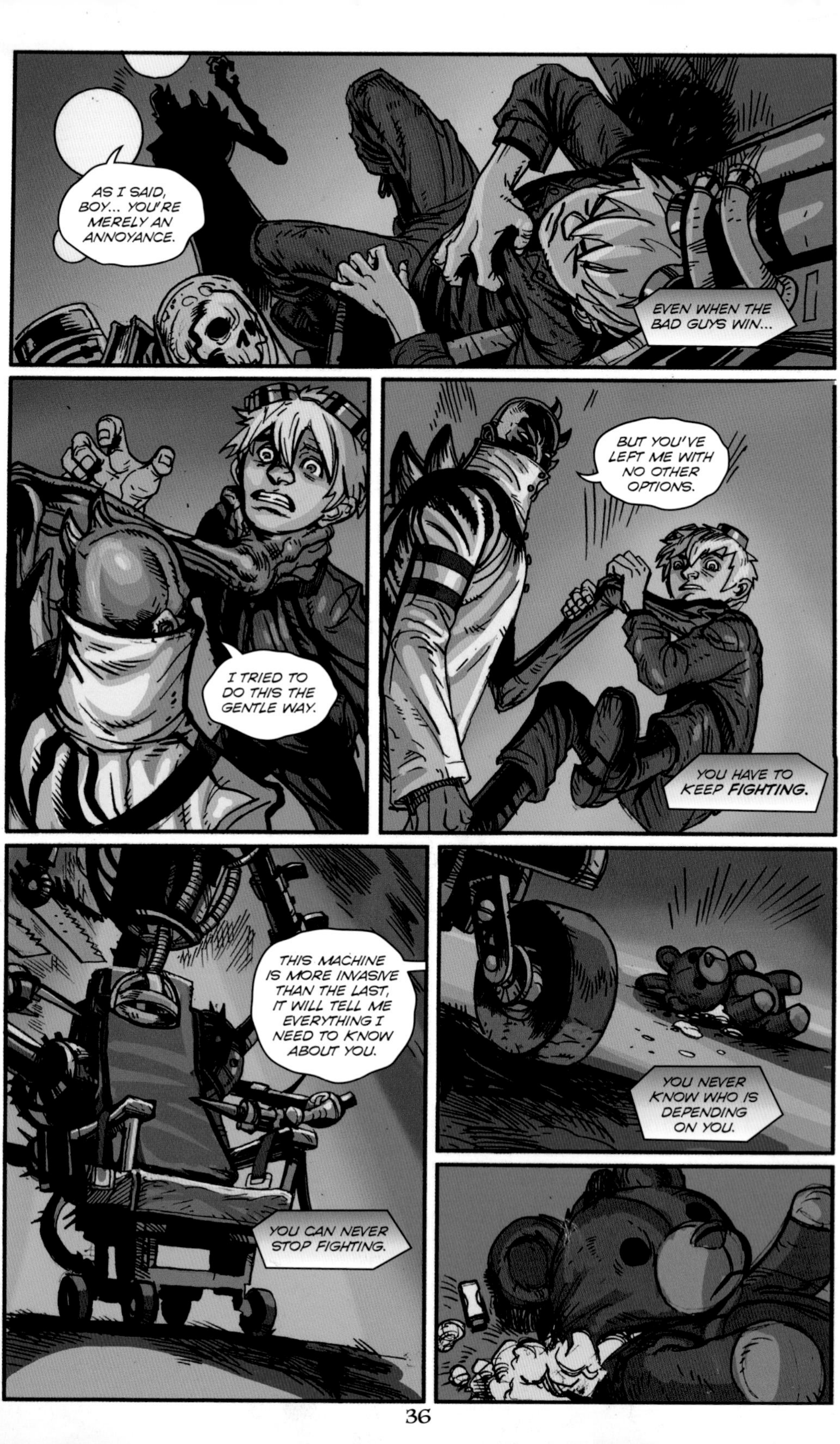
AS I SAID, BOY... YOU'RE MERELY AN ANNOYANCE.
EVEN WHEN THE BAD GUYS WIN...
I TRIED TO DO THIS THE GENTLE WAY.
BUT YOU'VE LEFT ME WITH NO OTHER OPTIONS.
YOU HAVE TO KEEP FIGHTING.
THIS MACHINE IS MORE INVASIVE THAN THE LAST, IT WILL TELL ME EVERYTHING I NEED TO KNOW ABOUT YOU.
YOU CAN NEVER STOP FIGHTING.
YOU NEVER KNOW WHO IS DEPENDING ON YOU.

CHAPTER SIX

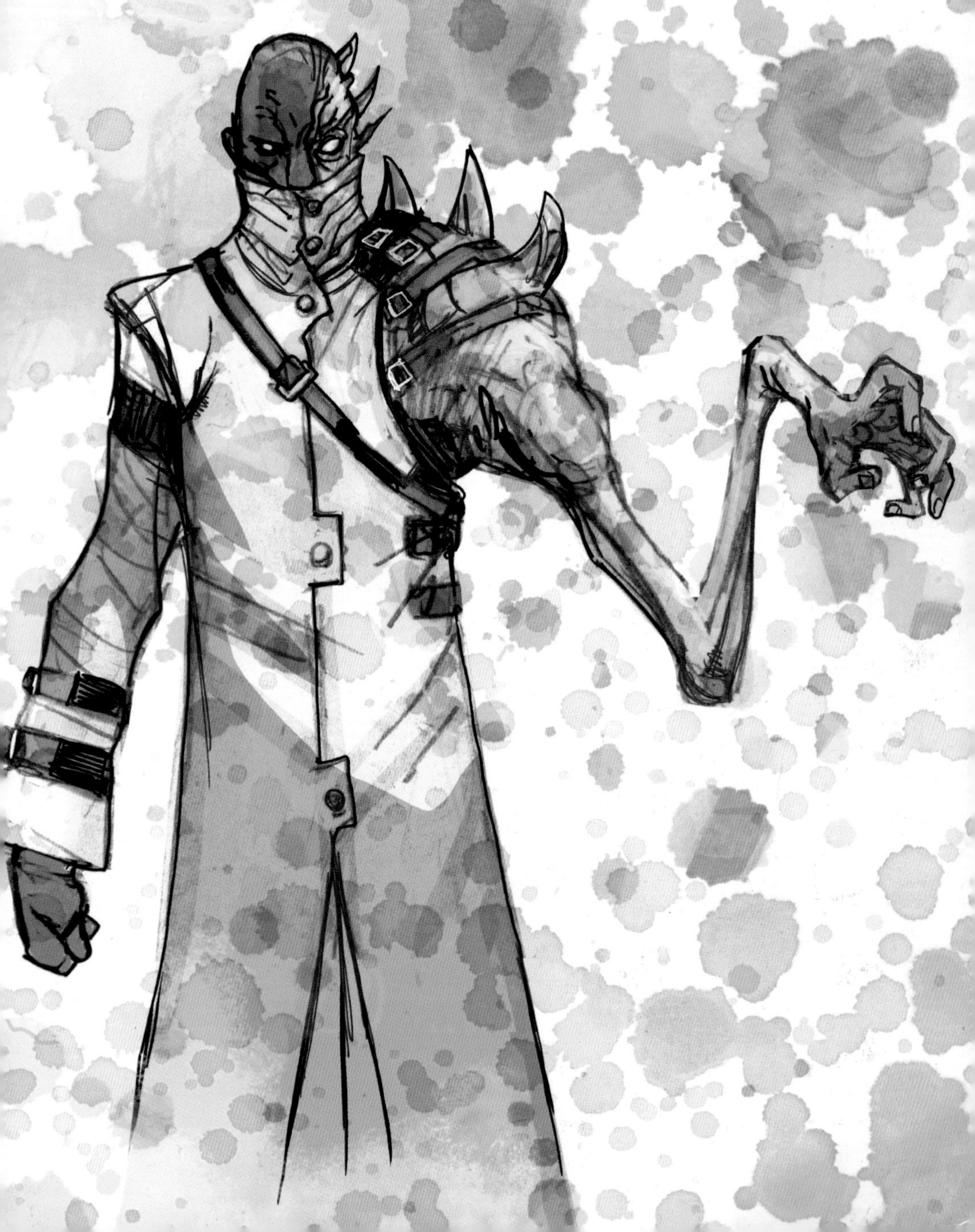

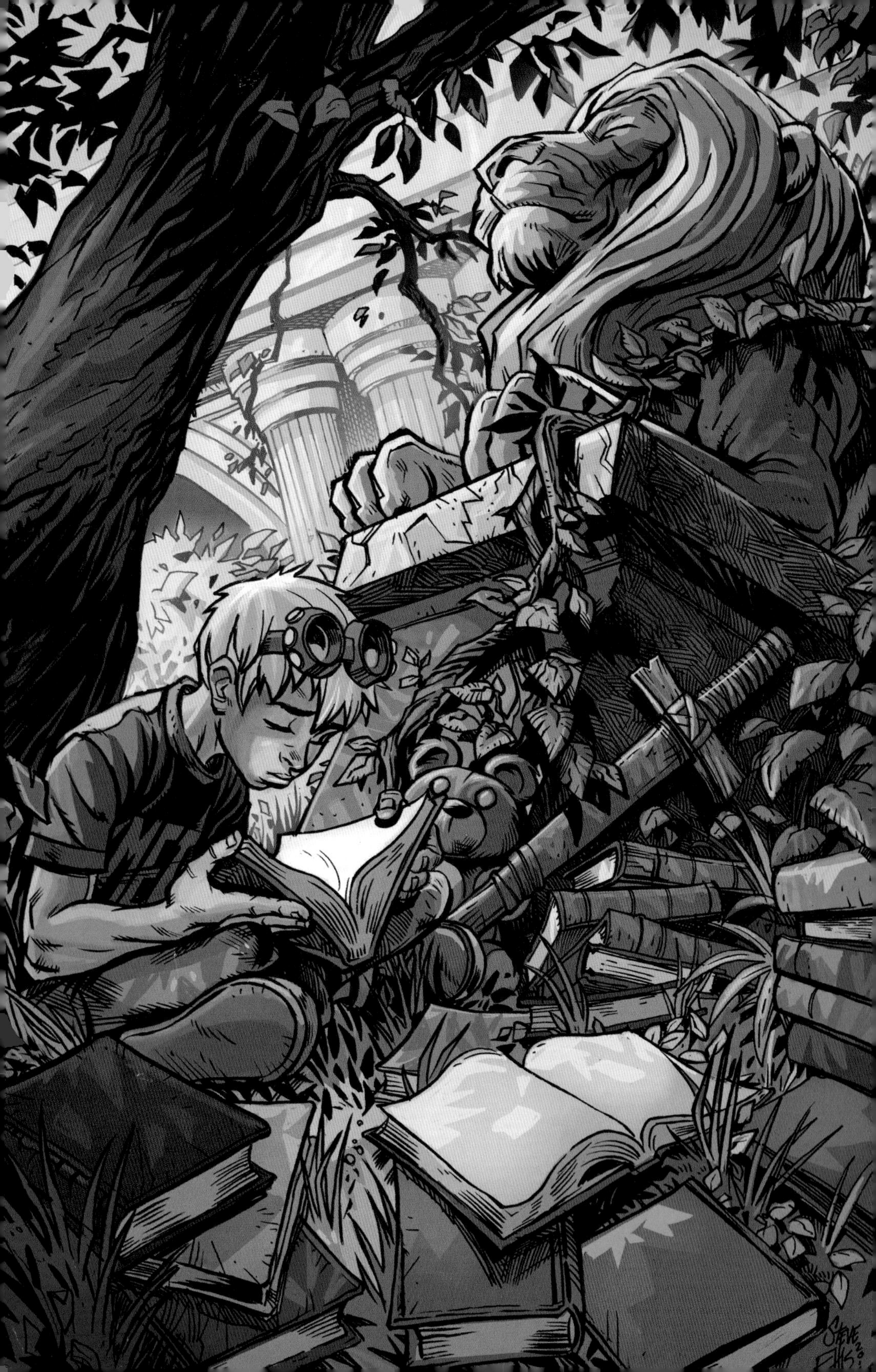

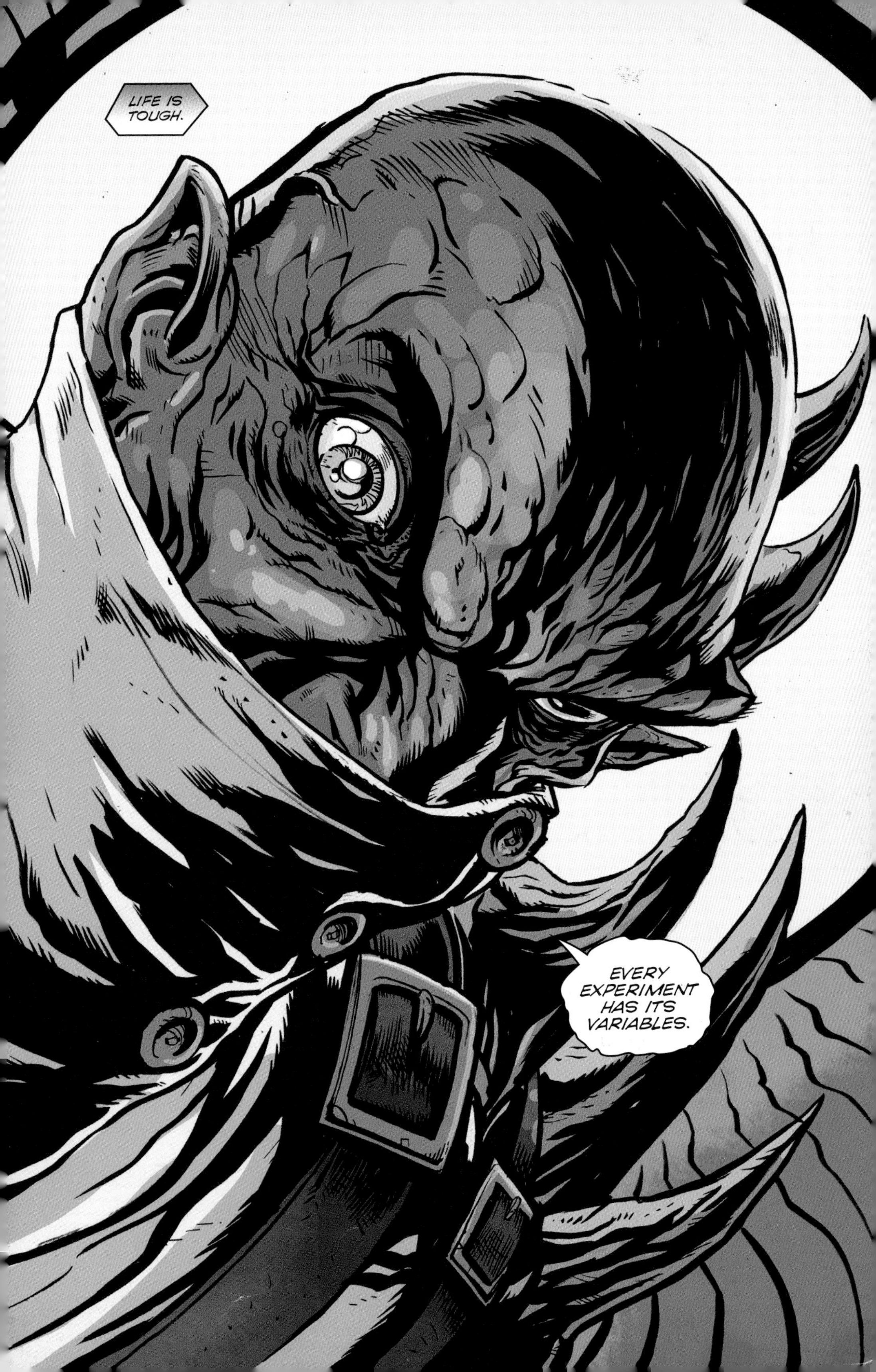
LIFE IS TOUGH.
EVERY EXPERIMENT HAS ITS VARIABLES.

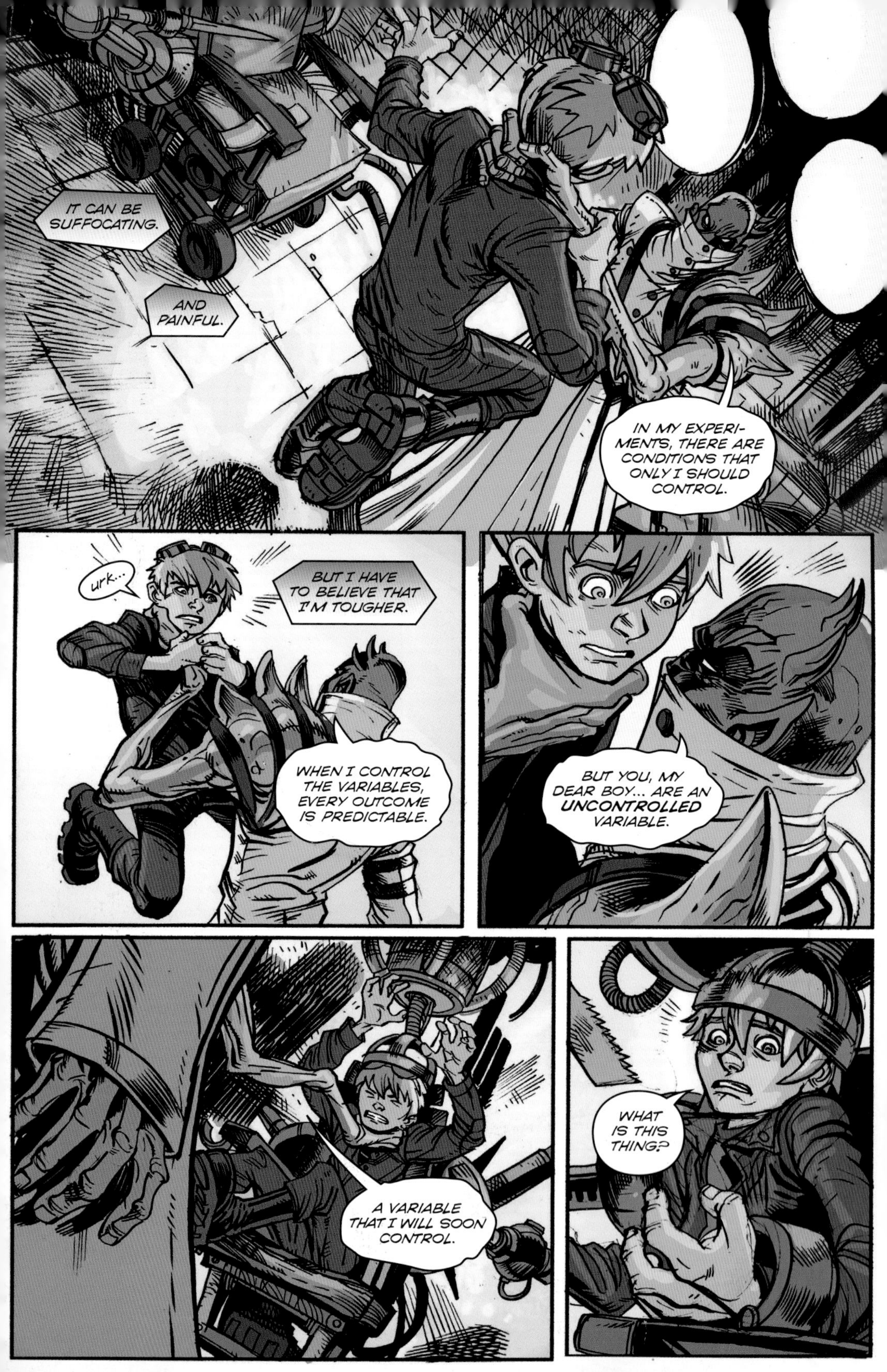
IT CAN BE SUFFOCATING.
AND PAINFUL.
IN MY EXPERI-MENTS, THERE ARE CONDITIONS THAT ONLY I SHOULD CONTROL.
urk...
BUT I HAVE TO BELIEVE THAT I'M TOUGHER.
WHEN I CONTROL THE VARIABLES, EVERY OUTCOME IS PREDICTABLE.
BUT YOU, MY DEAR BOY... ARE AN **UNCONTROLLED** VARIABLE.
A VARIABLE THAT I WILL SOON CONTROL.
WHAT IS THIS THING?

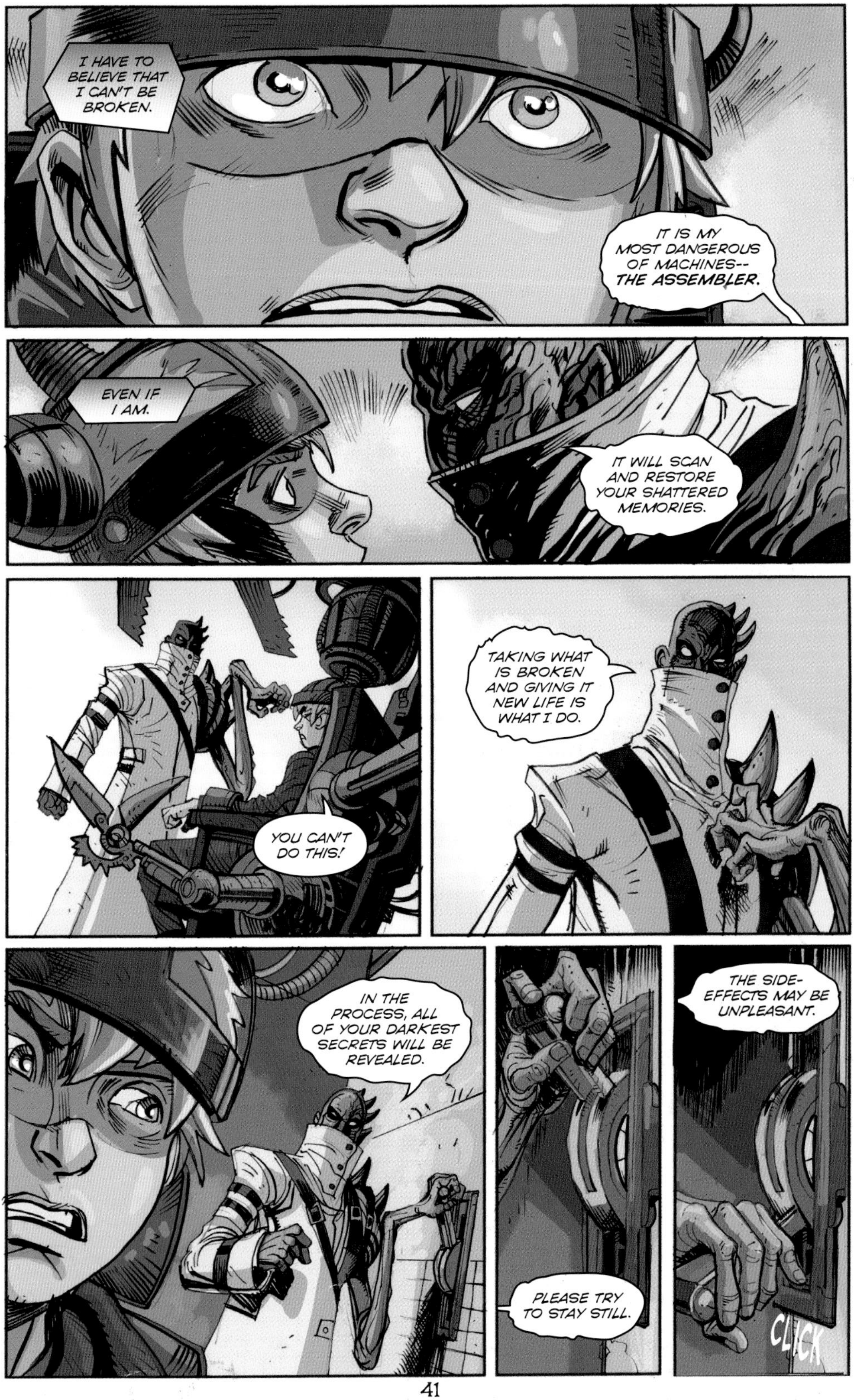
I HAVE TO BELIEVE THAT I CAN'T BE BROKEN.
IT IS MY MOST DANGEROUS OF MACHINES-- THE ASSEMBLER.
EVEN IF I AM.
IT WILL SCAN AND RESTORE YOUR SHATTERED MEMORIES.
YOU CAN'T DO THIS!
TAKING WHAT IS BROKEN AND GIVING IT NEW LIFE IS WHAT I DO.
IN THE PROCESS, ALL OF YOUR DARKEST SECRETS WILL BE REVEALED.
PLEASE TRY TO STAY STILL.
THE SIDE-EFFECTS MAY BE UNPLEASANT.
CLICK

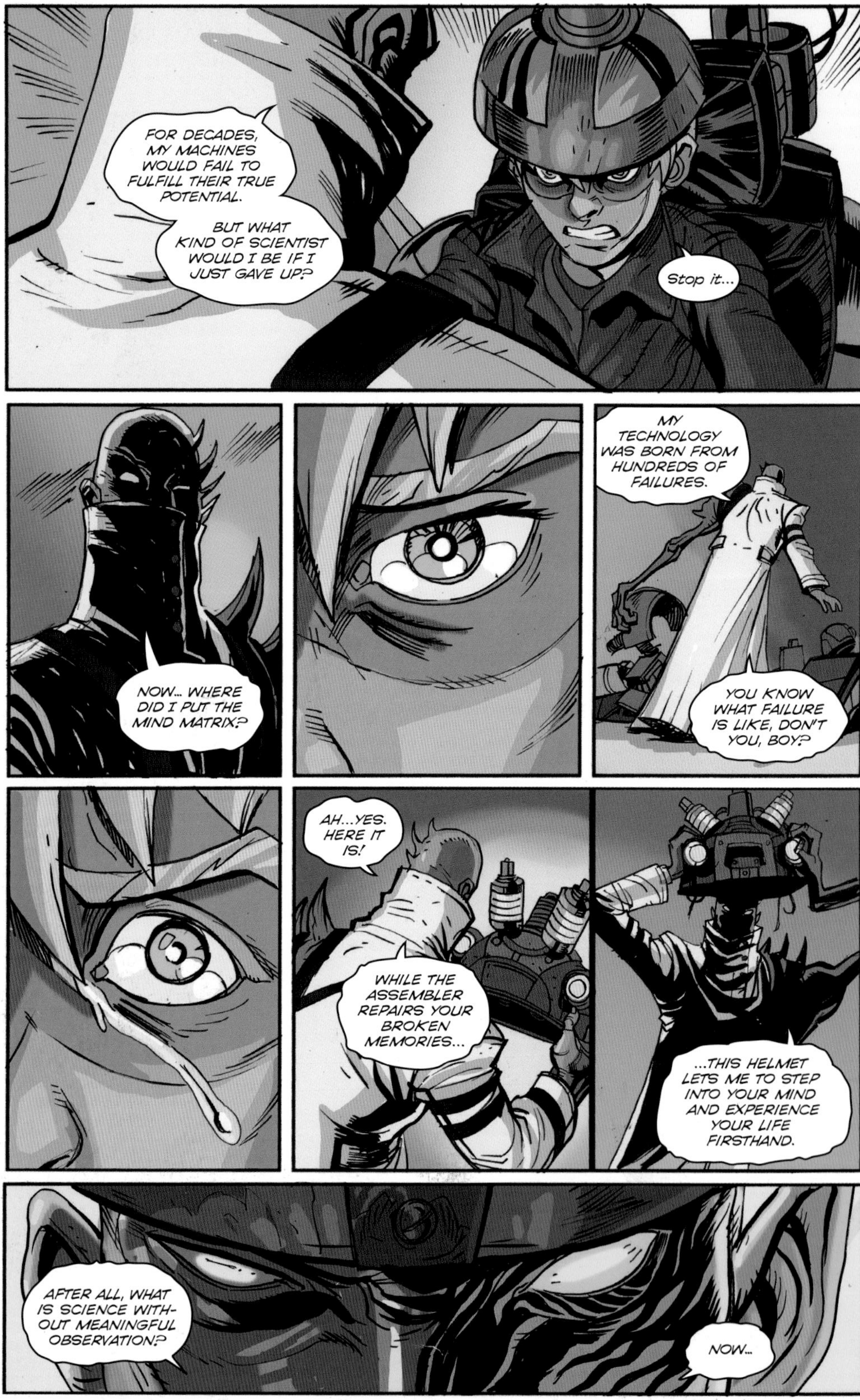
FOR DECADES, MY MACHINES WOULD FAIL TO FULFILL THEIR TRUE POTENTIAL.
BUT WHAT KIND OF SCIENTIST WOULD I BE IF I JUST GAVE UP?
Stop it...
NOW... WHERE DID I PUT THE MIND MATRIX?
MY TECHNOLOGY WAS BORN FROM HUNDREDS OF FAILURES.
YOU KNOW WHAT FAILURE IS LIKE, DON'T YOU, BOY?
AH...YES. HERE IT IS!
WHILE THE ASSEMBLER REPAIRS YOUR BROKEN MEMORIES...
...THIS HELMET LETS ME TO STEP INTO YOUR MIND AND EXPERIENCE YOUR LIFE FIRSTHAND.
AFTER ALL, WHAT IS SCIENCE WITH-OUT MEANINGFUL OBSERVATION?
NOW...

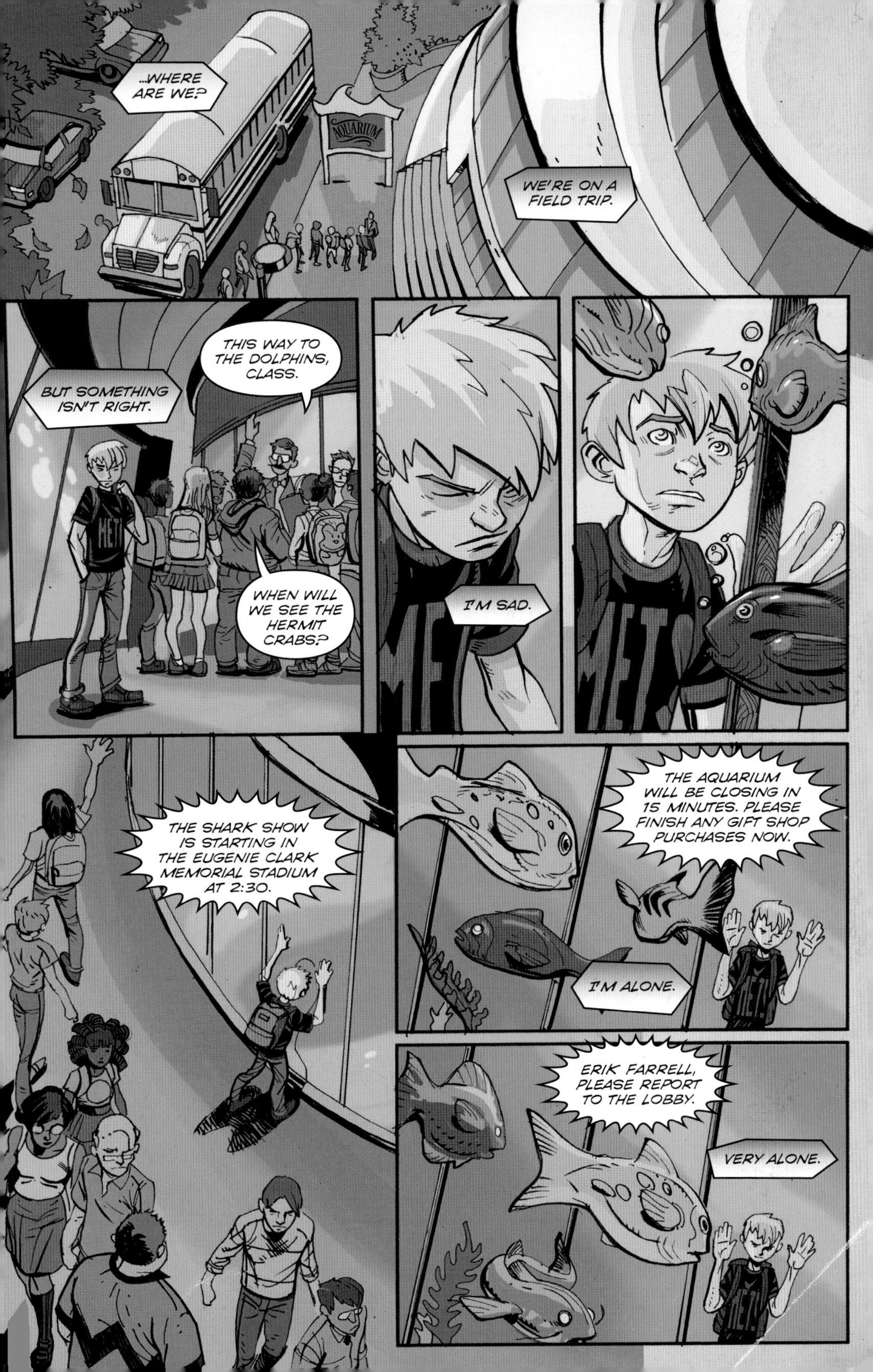
...WHERE ARE WE?
AQUARIUM
WE'RE ON A FIELD TRIP.
BUT SOMETHING ISN'T RIGHT.
THIS WAY TO THE DOLPHINS, CLASS.
WHEN WILL WE SEE THE HERMIT CRABS?
I'M SAD.
THE SHARK SHOW IS STARTING IN THE EUGENIE CLARK MEMORIAL STADIUM AT 2:30.
THE AQUARIUM WILL BE CLOSING IN 15 MINUTES. PLEASE FINISH ANY GIFT SHOP PURCHASES NOW.
I'M ALONE.
ERIK FARRELL, PLEASE REPORT TO THE LOBBY.
VERY ALONE.

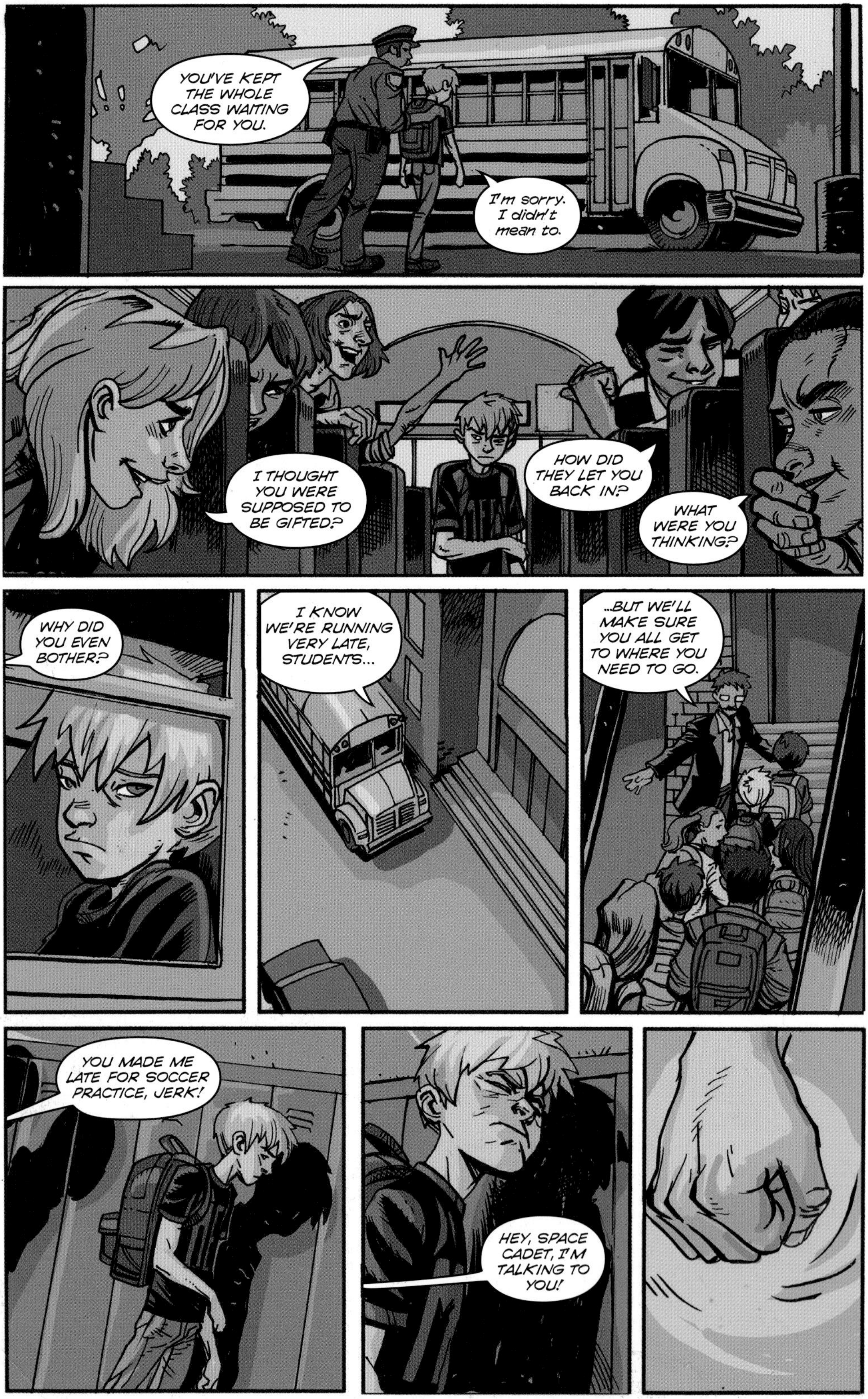
YOU'VE KEPT THE WHOLE CLASS WAITING FOR YOU.
I'm sorry. I didn't mean to.
I THOUGHT YOU WERE SUPPOSED TO BE GIFTED?
HOW DID THEY LET YOU BACK IN?
WHAT WERE YOU THINKING?
WHY DID YOU EVEN BOTHER?
I KNOW WE'RE RUNNING VERY LATE, STUDENTS...
...BUT WE'LL MAKE SURE YOU ALL GET TO WHERE YOU NEED TO GO.
YOU MADE ME LATE FOR SOCCER PRACTICE, JERK!
HEY, SPACE CADET, I'M TALKING TO YOU!

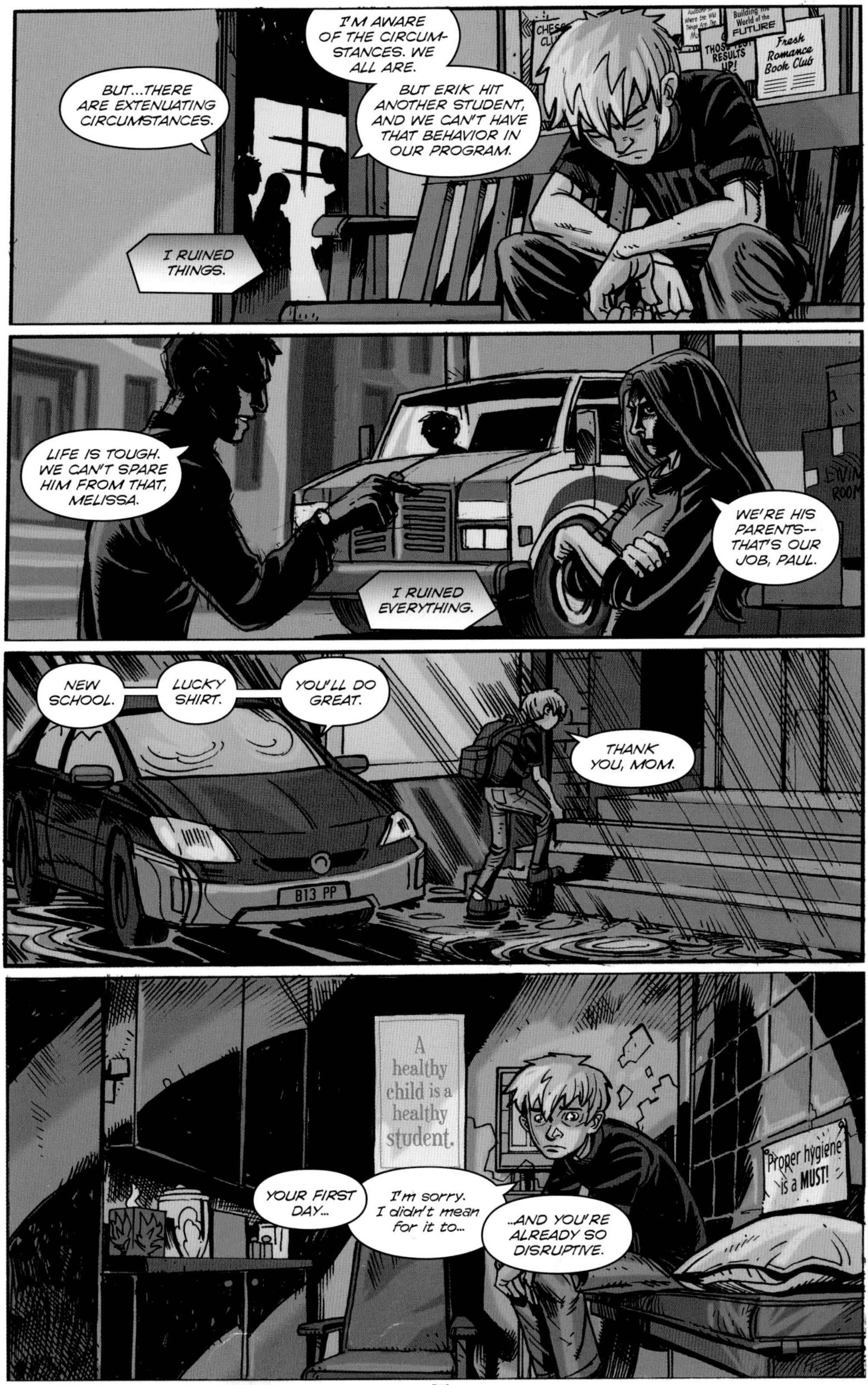
Building the World of the FUTURE
Fresh Romance Book Club
BUT...THERE ARE EXTENUATING CIRCUMSTANCES.
I'M AWARE OF THE CIRCUMSTANCES. WE ALL ARE.
BUT ERIK HIT ANOTHER STUDENT, AND WE CAN'T HAVE THAT BEHAVIOR IN OUR PROGRAM.
I RUINED THINGS.
LIFE IS TOUGH. WE CAN'T SPARE HIM FROM THAT, MELISSA.
WE'RE HIS PARENTS-- THAT'S OUR JOB, PAUL.
I RUINED EVERYTHING.
NEW SCHOOL.
LUCKY SHIRT.
YOU'LL DO GREAT.
THANK YOU, MOM.
B13 PP
A healthy child is a healthy student.
Proper hygiene is a MUST!
YOUR FIRST DAY...
I'm sorry. I didn't mean for it to...
...AND YOU'RE ALREADY SO DISRUPTIVE.

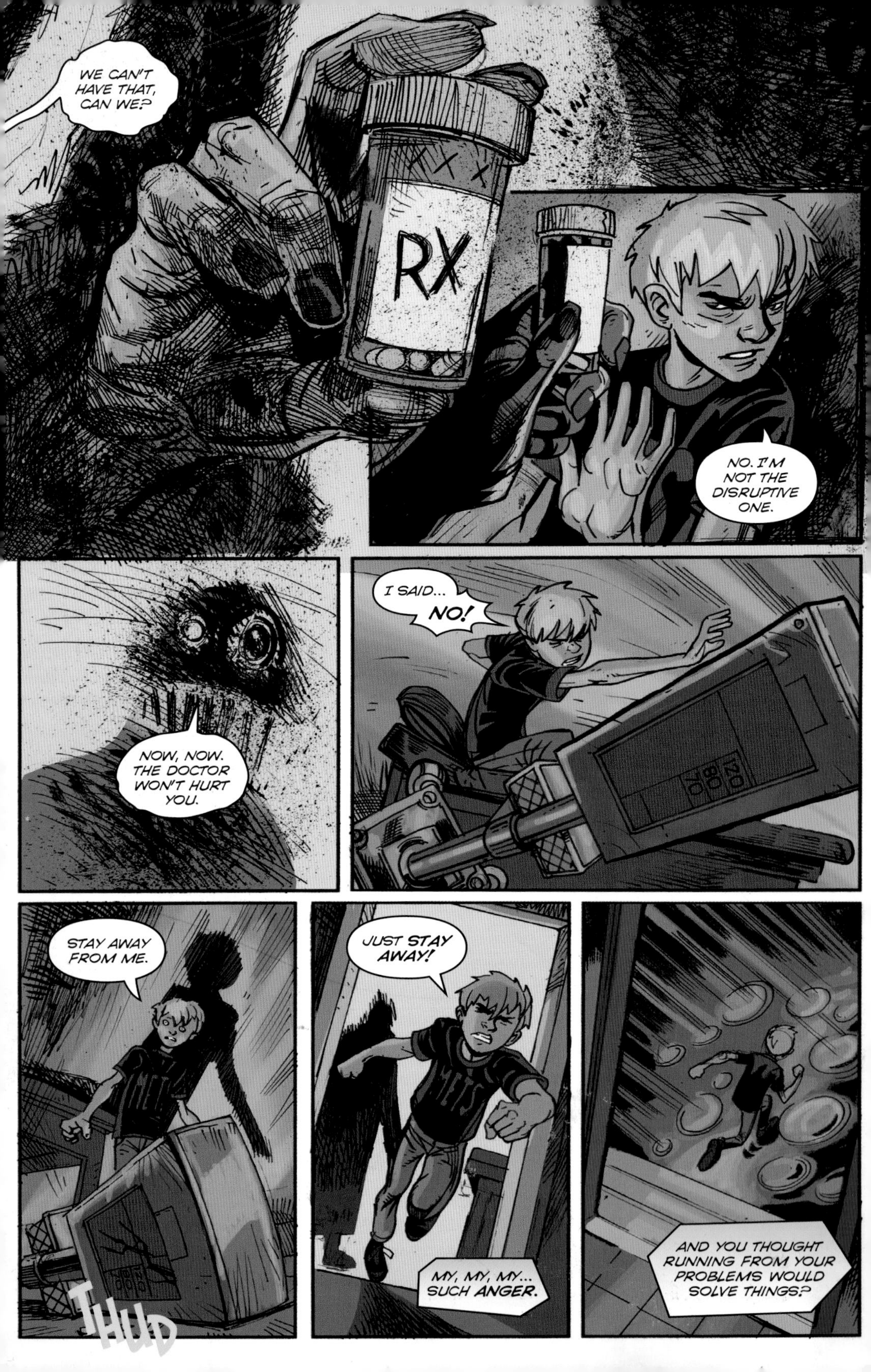
WE CAN'T HAVE THAT, CAN WE?
RX
NO. I'M NOT THE DISRUPTIVE ONE.
NOW, NOW. THE DOCTOR WON'T HURT YOU.
I SAID... NO!
120 80 70
STAY AWAY FROM ME.
THUD
JUST STAY AWAY!
MY, MY, MY... SUCH ANGER.
AND YOU THOUGHT RUNNING FROM YOUR PROBLEMS WOULD SOLVE THINGS?

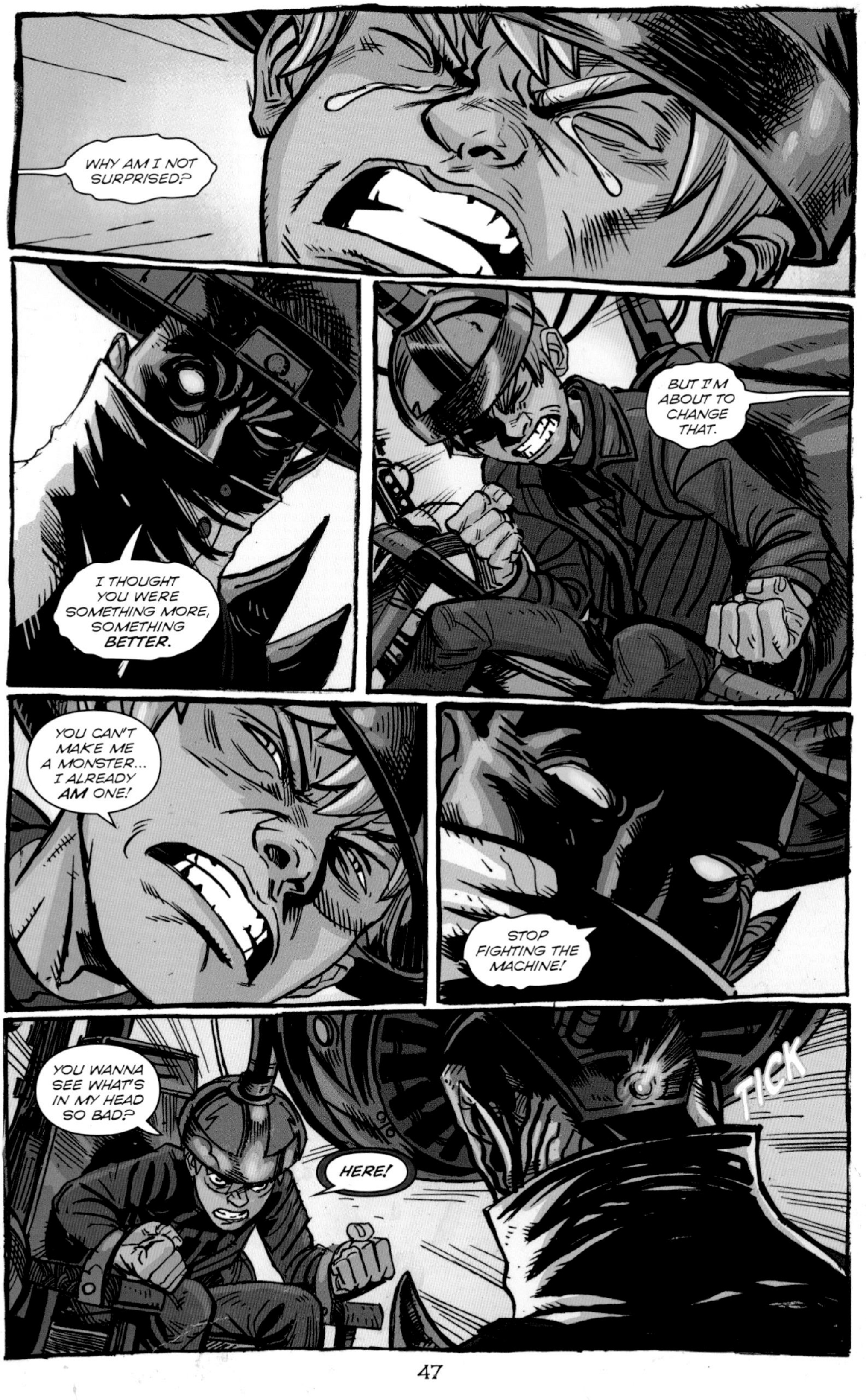
WHY AM I NOT SURPRISED?
BUT I'M ABOUT TO CHANGE THAT.
I THOUGHT YOU WERE SOMETHING MORE, SOMETHING BETTER.
YOU CAN'T MAKE ME A MONSTER... I ALREADY AM ONE!
STOP FIGHTING THE MACHINE!
YOU WANNA SEE WHAT'S IN MY HEAD SO BAD?
HERE!
TICK

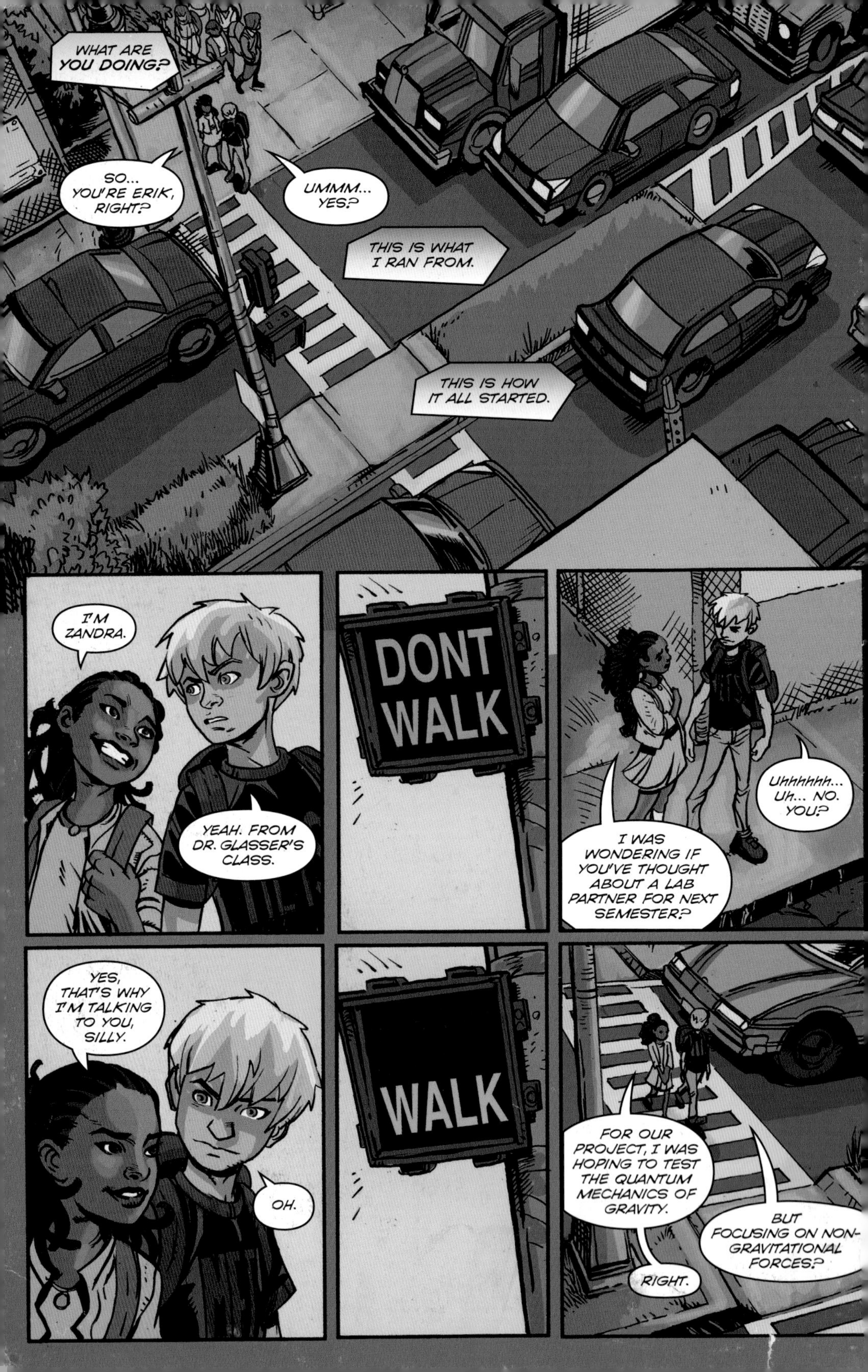
WHAT ARE YOU DOING?
SO... YOU'RE ERIK, RIGHT?
UMMM... YES?
THIS IS WHAT I RAN FROM.
THIS IS HOW IT ALL STARTED.
I'M ZANDRA.
YEAH. FROM DR. GLASSER'S CLASS.
DONT WALK
I WAS WONDERING IF YOU'VE THOUGHT ABOUT A LAB PARTNER FOR NEXT SEMESTER?
Uhhhhhh... Uh... NO. YOU?
YES, THAT'S WHY I'M TALKING TO YOU, SILLY.
OH.
WALK
FOR OUR PROJECT, I WAS HOPING TO TEST THE QUANTUM MECHANICS OF GRAVITY.
RIGHT.
BUT FOCUSING ON NON-GRAVITATIONAL FORCES?

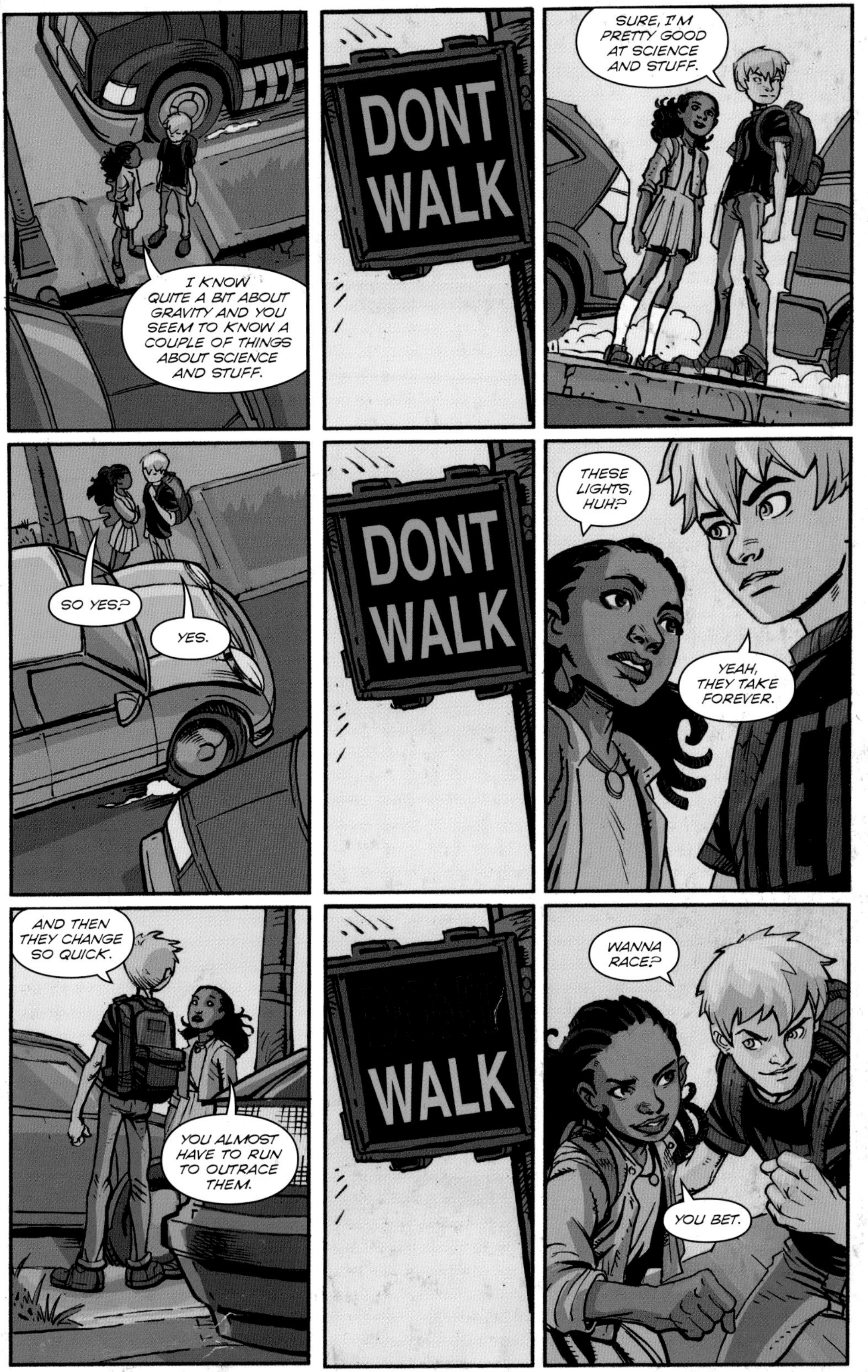
I KNOW QUITE A BIT ABOUT GRAVITY AND YOU SEEM TO KNOW A COUPLE OF THINGS ABOUT SCIENCE AND STUFF.
DONT WALK
SURE, I'M PRETTY GOOD AT SCIENCE AND STUFF.
SO YES?
YES.
DONT WALK
THESE LIGHTS, HUH?
YEAH, THEY TAKE FOREVER.
AND THEN THEY CHANGE SO QUICK.
YOU ALMOST HAVE TO RUN TO OUTRACE THEM.
WALK
WANNA RACE?
YOU BET.

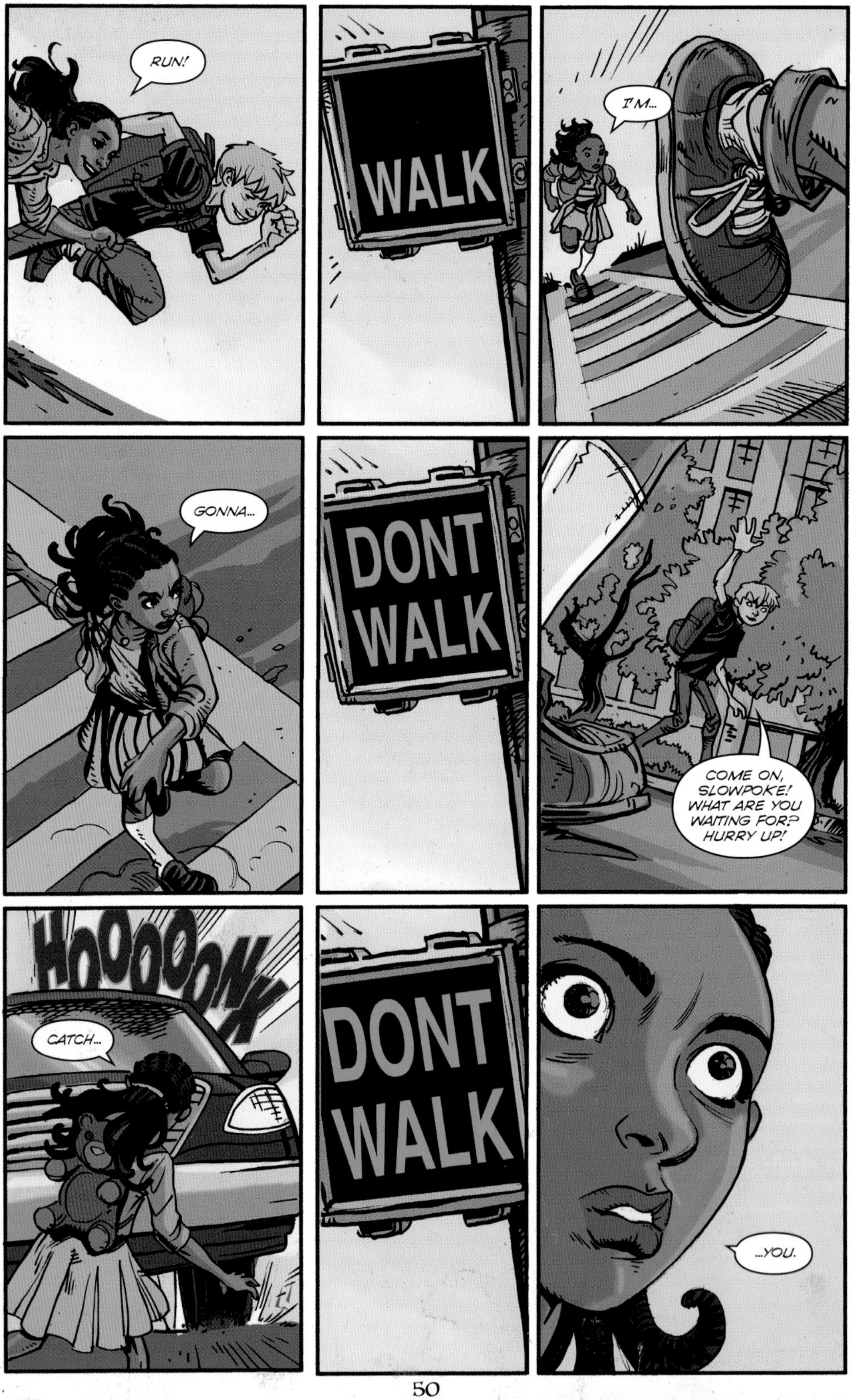
RUN!
WALK
I'M...
GONNA...
DONT WALK
COME ON, SLOWPOKE! WHAT ARE YOU WAITING FOR? HURRY UP!
HOOOOONK
CATCH...
DONT WALK
...YOU.

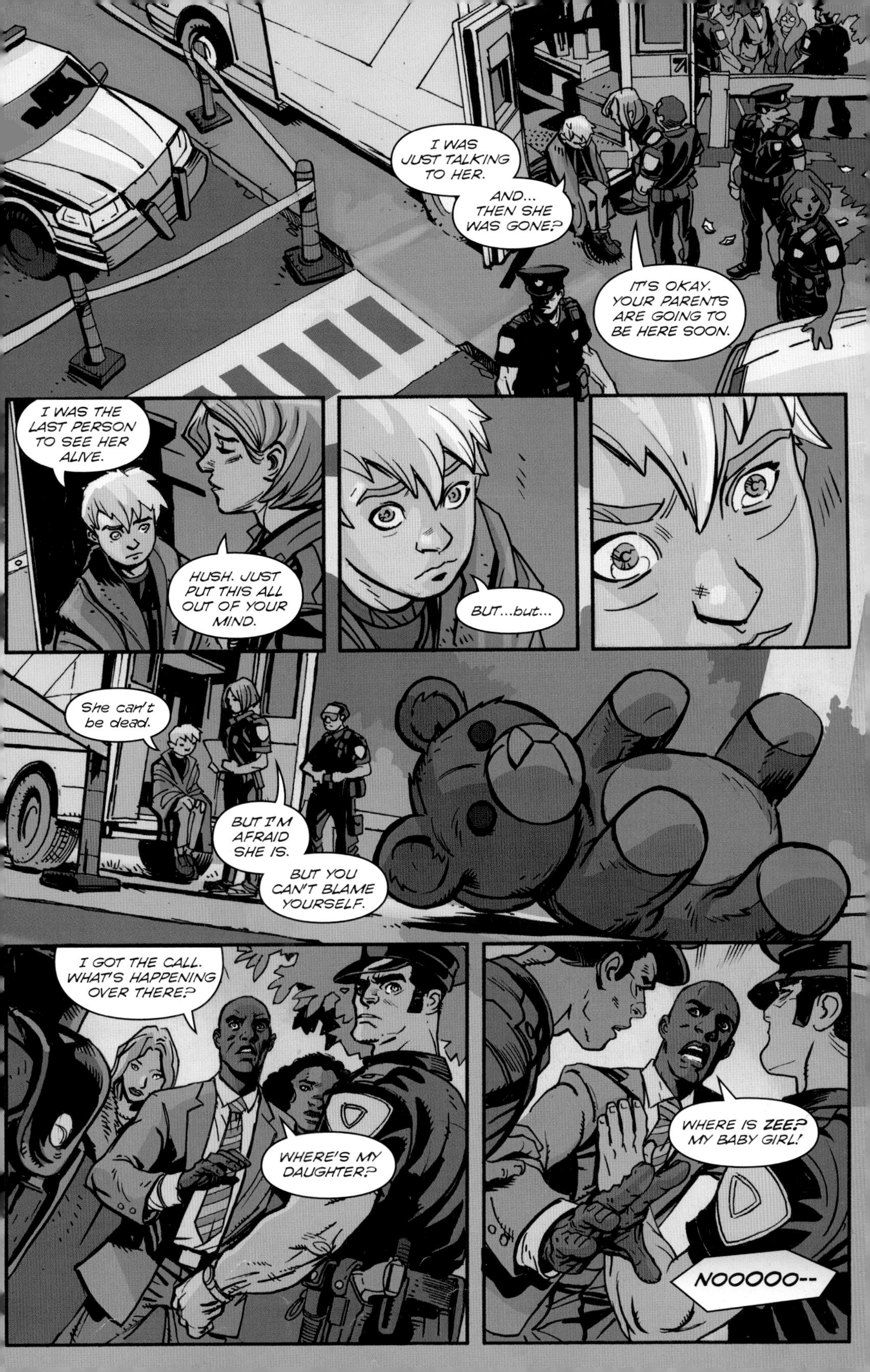
I WAS JUST TALKING TO HER.
AND... THEN SHE WAS GONE?
IT'S OKAY. YOUR PARENTS ARE GOING TO BE HERE SOON.
I WAS THE LAST PERSON TO SEE HER ALIVE.
HUSH. JUST PUT THIS ALL OUT OF YOUR MIND.
BUT...but...
She can't be dead.
BUT I'M AFRAID SHE IS.
BUT YOU CAN'T BLAME YOURSELF.
I GOT THE CALL. WHAT'S HAPPENING OVER THERE?
WHERE'S MY DAUGHTER?
WHERE IS ZEE? MY BABY GIRL!
NOOOOO--

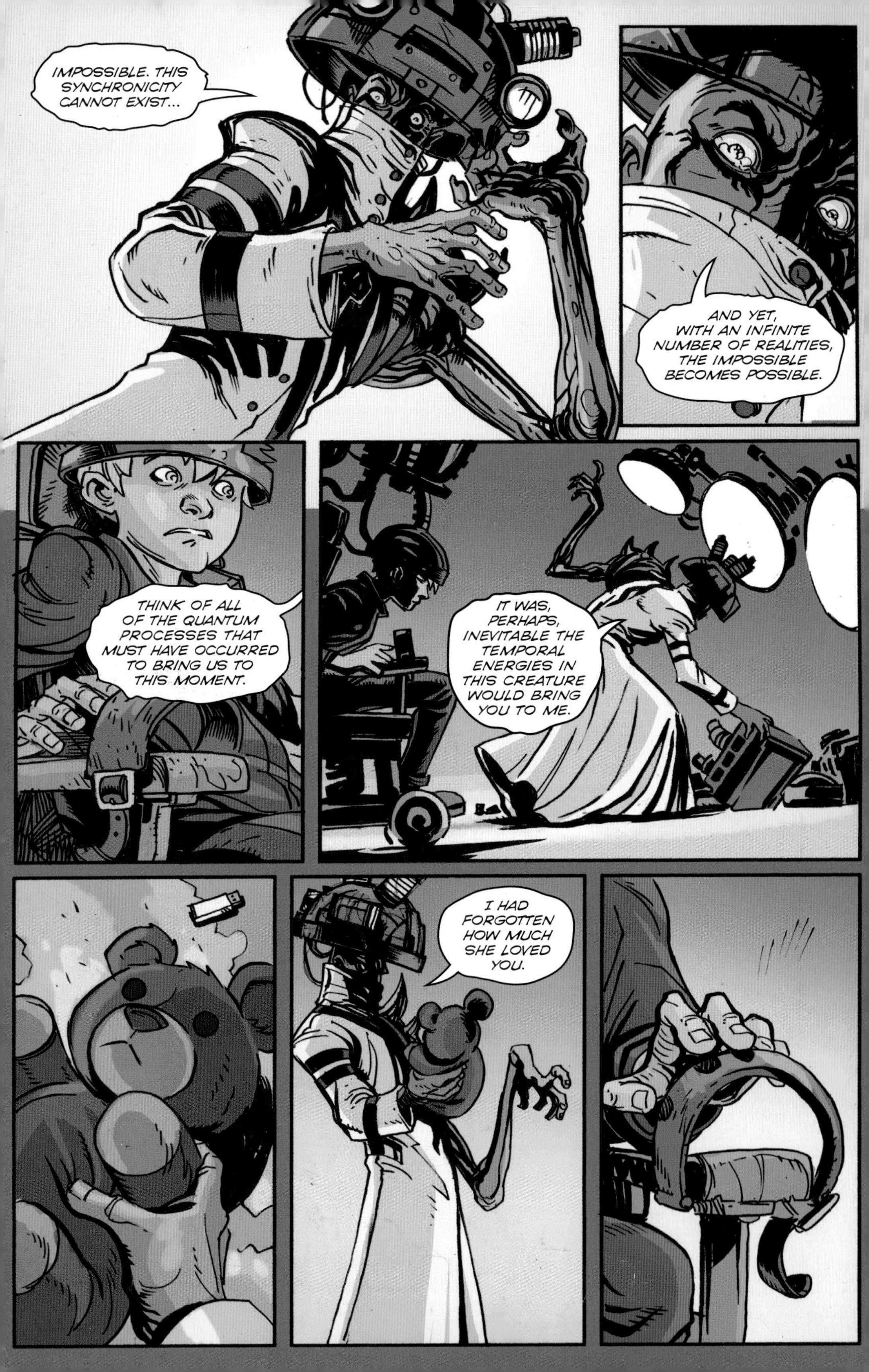
IMPOSSIBLE. THIS SYNCHRONICITY CANNOT EXIST...
AND YET, WITH AN INFINITE NUMBER OF REALITIES, THE IMPOSSIBLE BECOMES POSSIBLE.
THINK OF ALL OF THE QUANTUM PROCESSES THAT MUST HAVE OCCURRED TO BRING US TO THIS MOMENT.
IT WAS, PERHAPS, INEVITABLE THE TEMPORAL ENERGIES IN THIS CREATURE WOULD BRING YOU TO ME.
I HAD FORGOTTEN HOW MUCH SHE LOVED YOU.

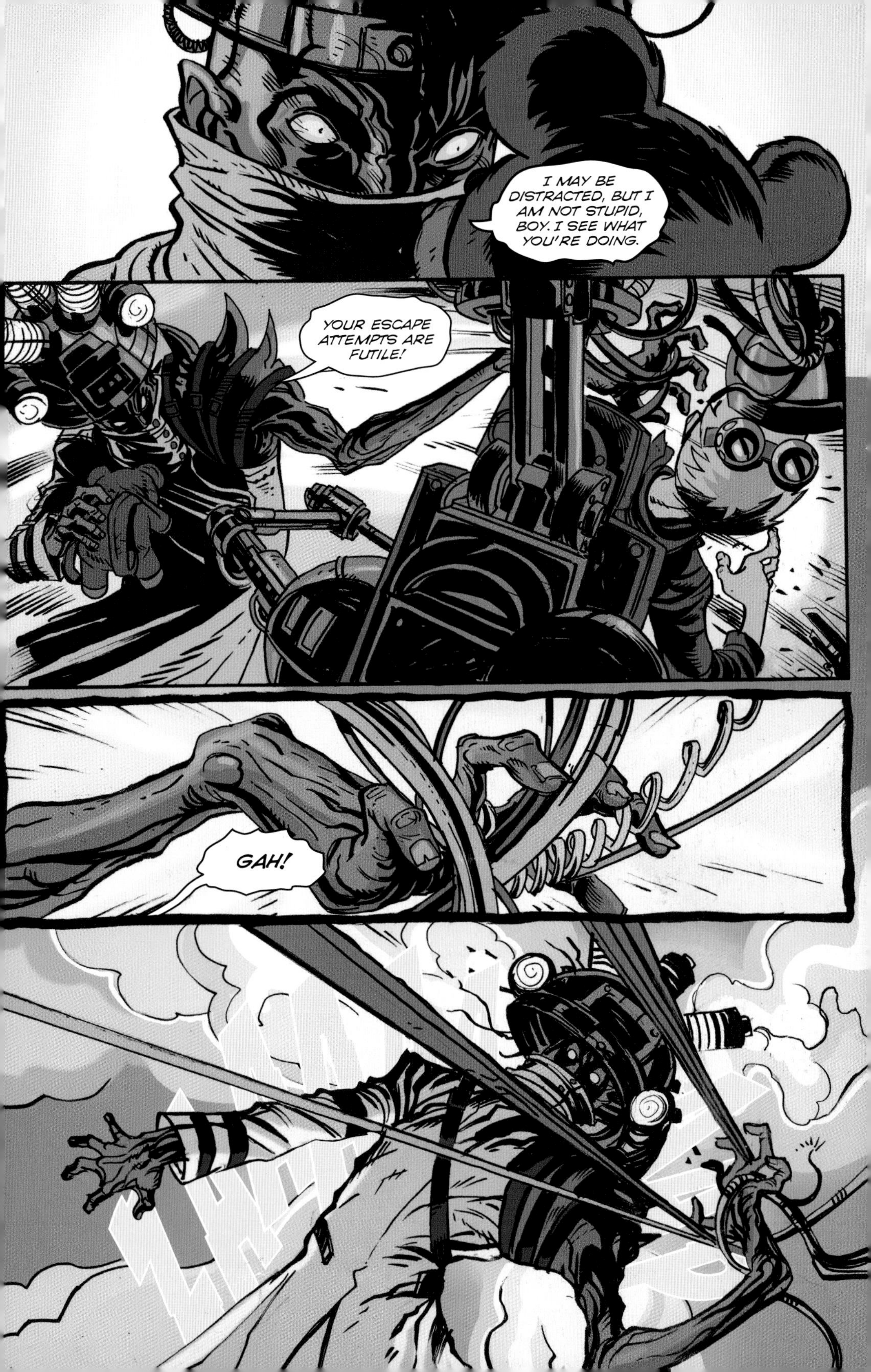
I MAY BE DISTRACTED, BUT I AM NOT STUPID, BOY. I SEE WHAT YOU'RE DOING.
YOUR ESCAPE ATTEMPTS ARE FUTILE!
GAH!

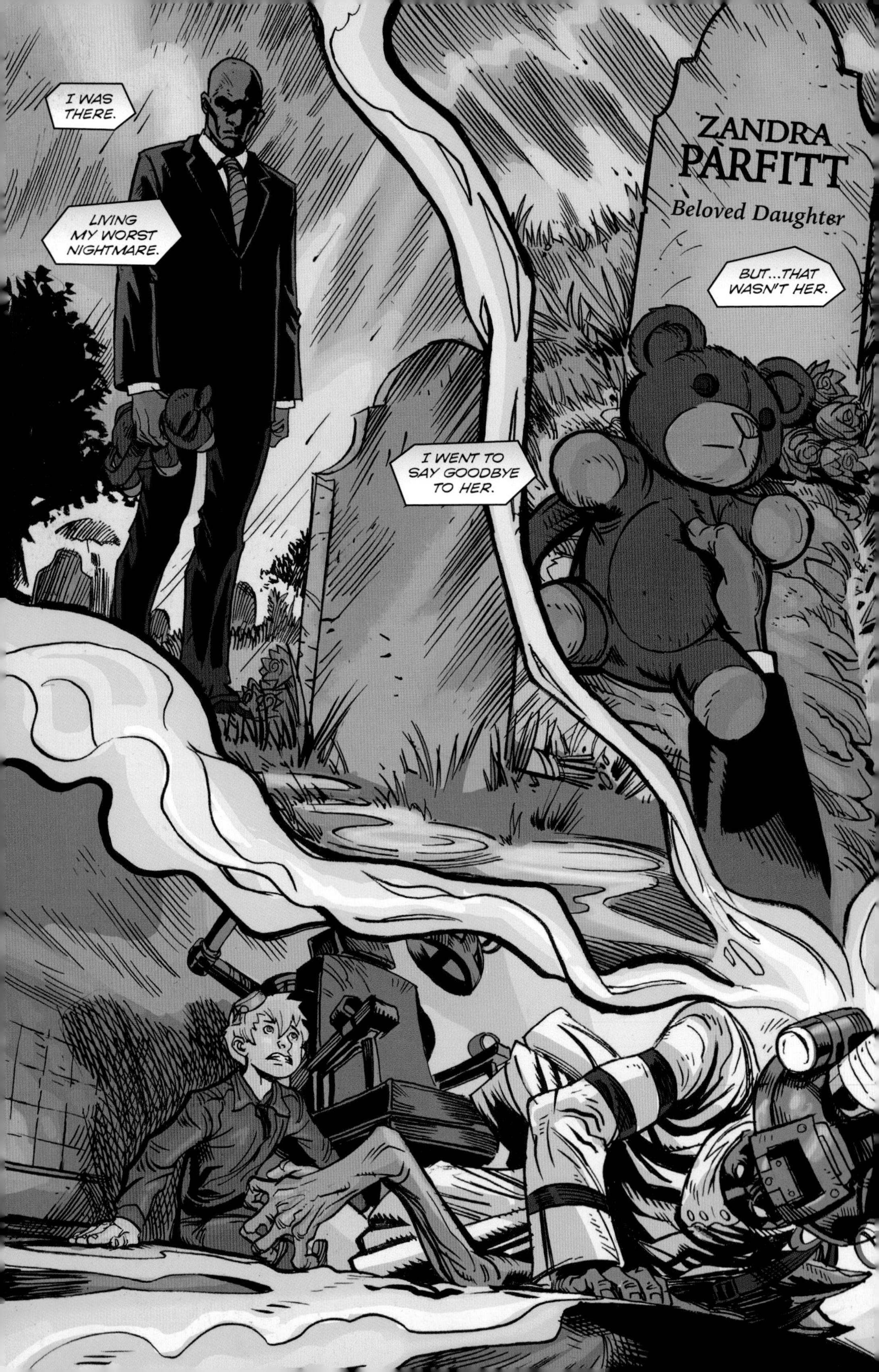
I WAS THERE.
LIVING MY WORST NIGHTMARE.
ZANDRA PARFITT
Beloved Daughter
BUT...THAT WASN'T HER.
I WENT TO SAY GOODBYE TO HER.

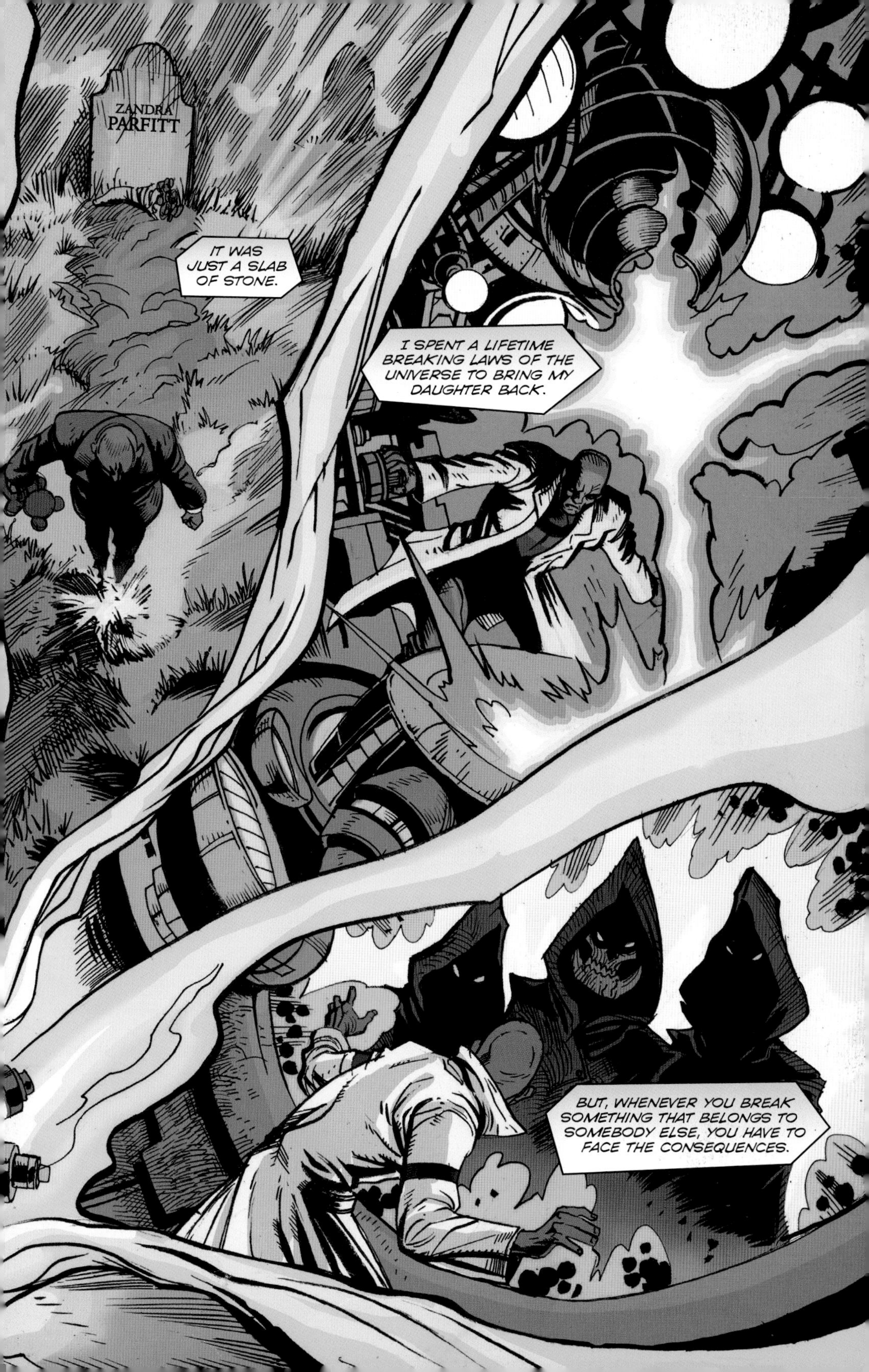
ZANDRA PARFITT
IT WAS JUST A SLAB OF STONE.
I SPENT A LIFETIME BREAKING LAWS OF THE UNIVERSE TO BRING MY DAUGHTER BACK.
BUT, WHENEVER YOU BREAK SOMETHING THAT BELONGS TO SOMEBODY ELSE, YOU HAVE TO FACE THE CONSEQUENCES.

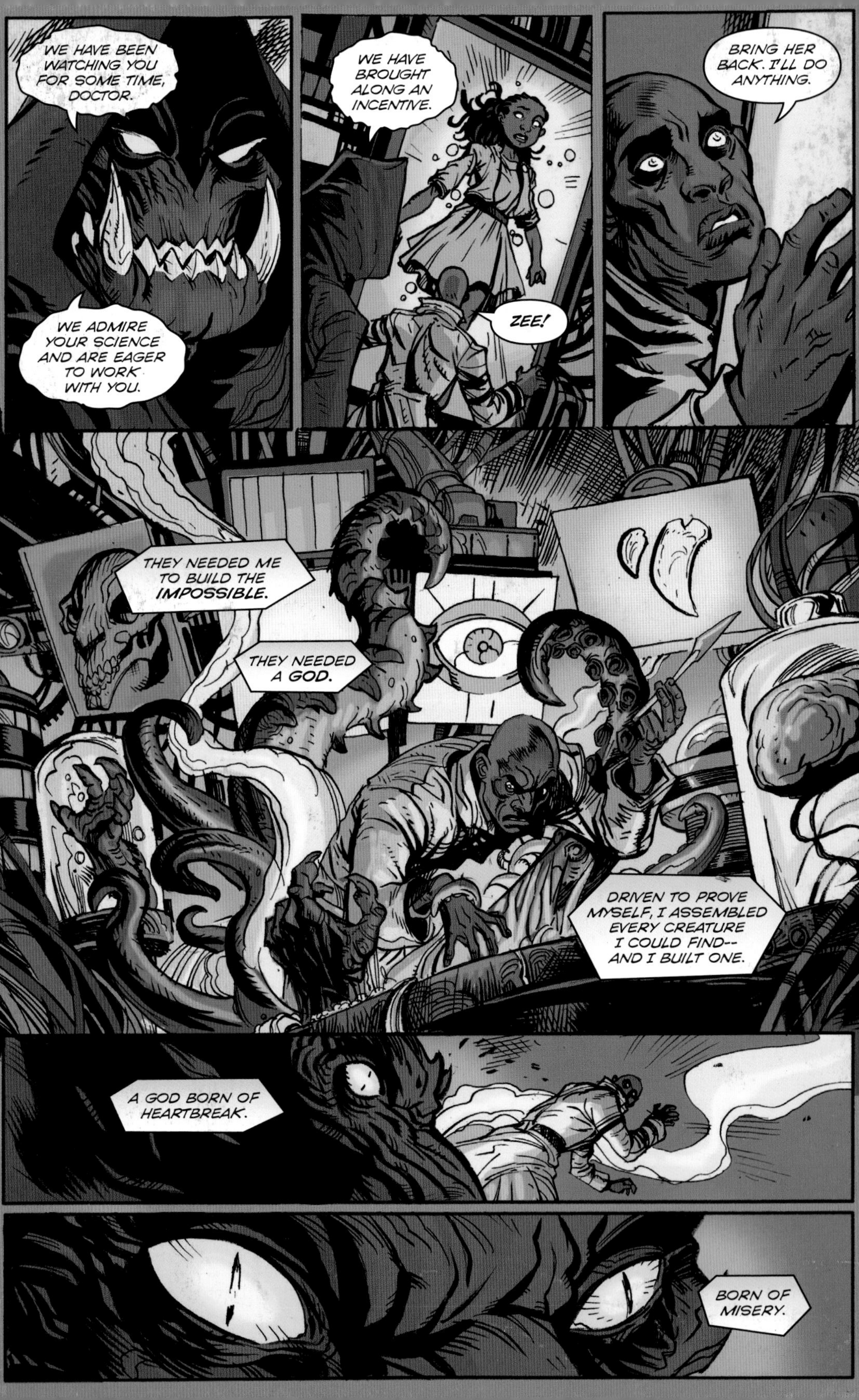
WE HAVE BEEN WATCHING YOU FOR SOME TIME, DOCTOR.
WE ADMIRE YOUR SCIENCE AND ARE EAGER TO WORK WITH YOU.
WE HAVE BROUGHT ALONG AN INCENTIVE.
ZEE!
BRING HER BACK. I'LL DO ANYTHING.
THEY NEEDED ME TO BUILD THE IMPOSSIBLE.
THEY NEEDED A GOD.
DRIVEN TO PROVE MYSELF, I ASSEMBLED EVERY CREATURE I COULD FIND-- AND I BUILT ONE.
A GOD BORN OF HEARTBREAK.
BORN OF MISERY.

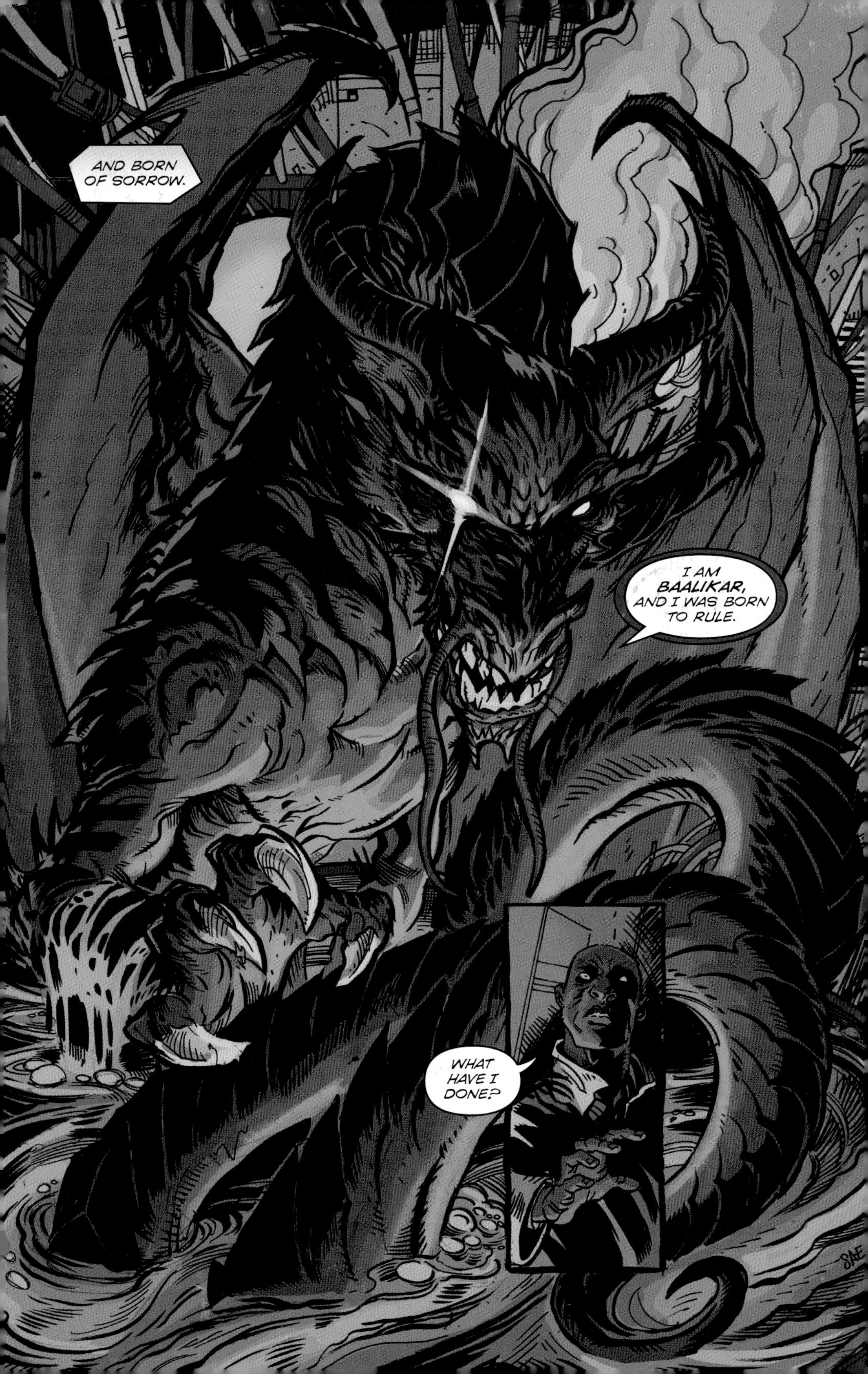
AND BORN OF SORROW.
I AM BAALIKAR, AND I WAS BORN TO RULE.
WHAT HAVE I DONE?

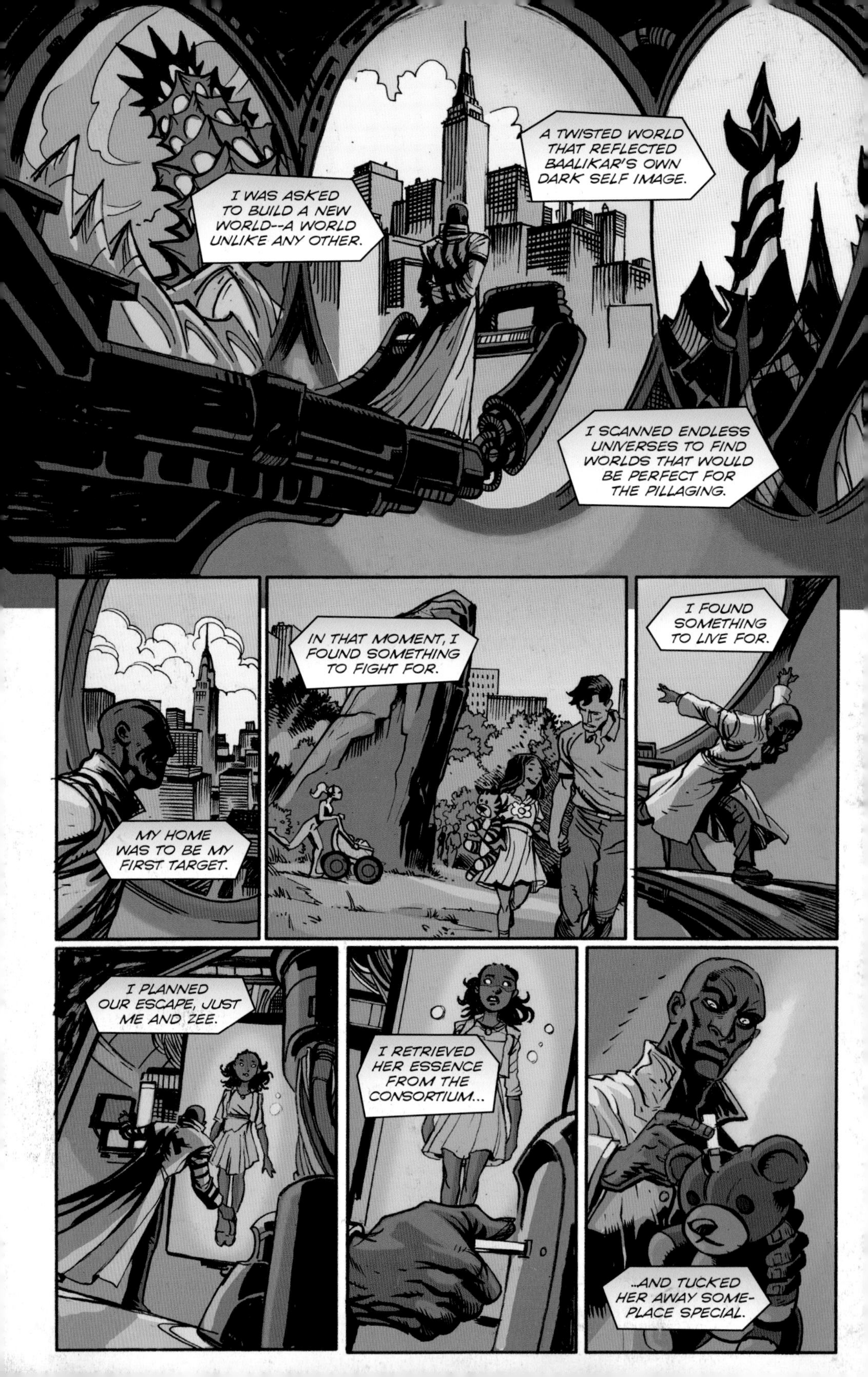
I WAS ASKED TO BUILD A NEW WORLD--A WORLD UNLIKE ANY OTHER.
A TWISTED WORLD THAT REFLECTED BAALIKAR'S OWN DARK SELF IMAGE.
I SCANNED ENDLESS UNIVERSES TO FIND WORLDS THAT WOULD BE PERFECT FOR THE PILLAGING.
MY HOME WAS TO BE MY FIRST TARGET.
IN THAT MOMENT, I FOUND SOMETHING TO FIGHT FOR.
I FOUND SOMETHING TO LIVE FOR.
I PLANNED OUR ESCAPE, JUST ME AND ZEE.
I RETRIEVED HER ESSENCE FROM THE CONSORTIUM...
...AND TUCKED HER AWAY SOME-PLACE SPECIAL.

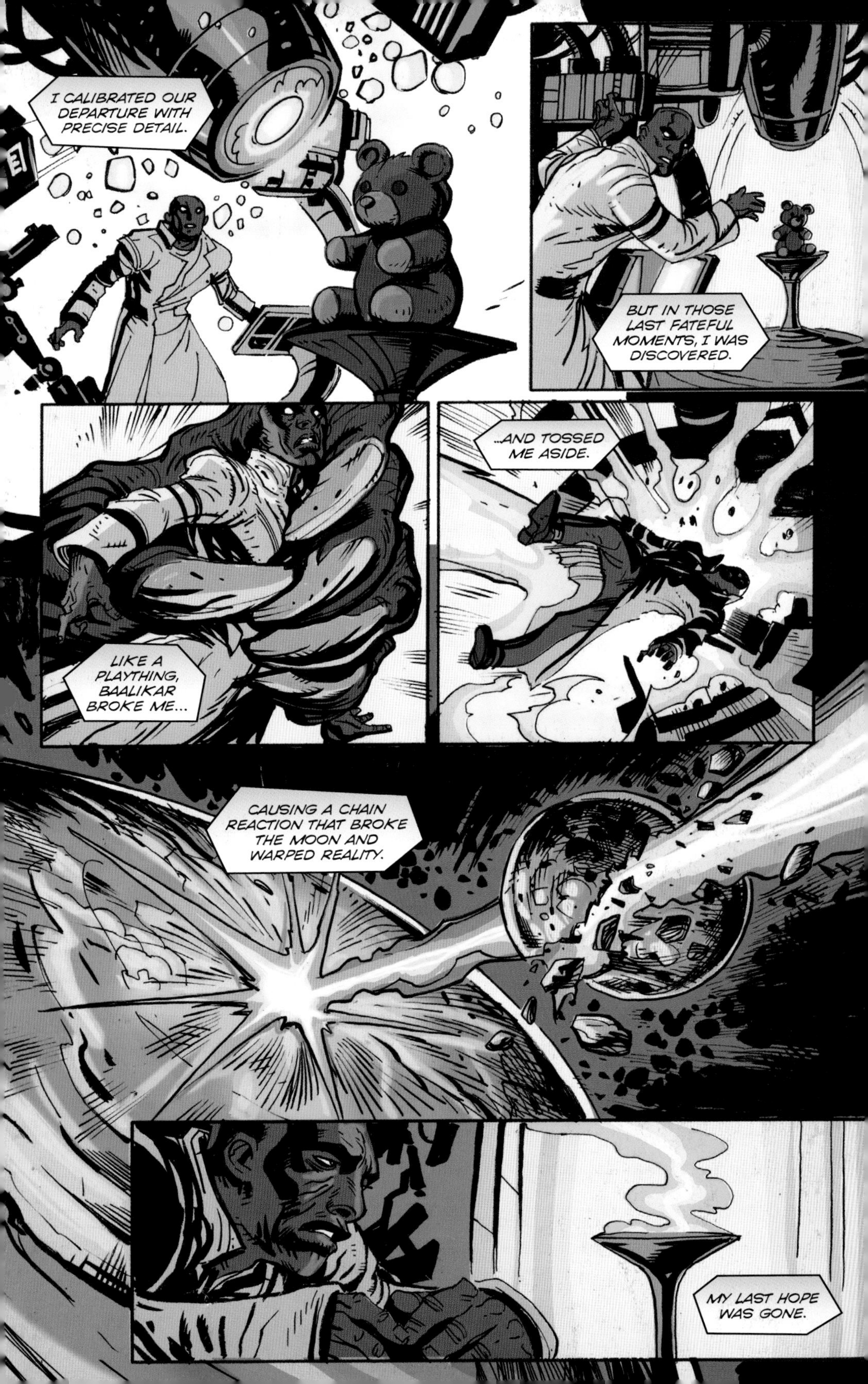
I CALIBRATED OUR DEPARTURE WITH PRECISE DETAIL.
BUT IN THOSE LAST FATEFUL MOMENTS, I WAS DISCOVERED.
LIKE A PLAYTHING, BAALIKAR BROKE ME...
...AND TOSSED ME ASIDE.
CAUSING A CHAIN REACTION THAT BROKE THE MOON AND WARPED REALITY.
MY LAST HOPE WAS GONE.

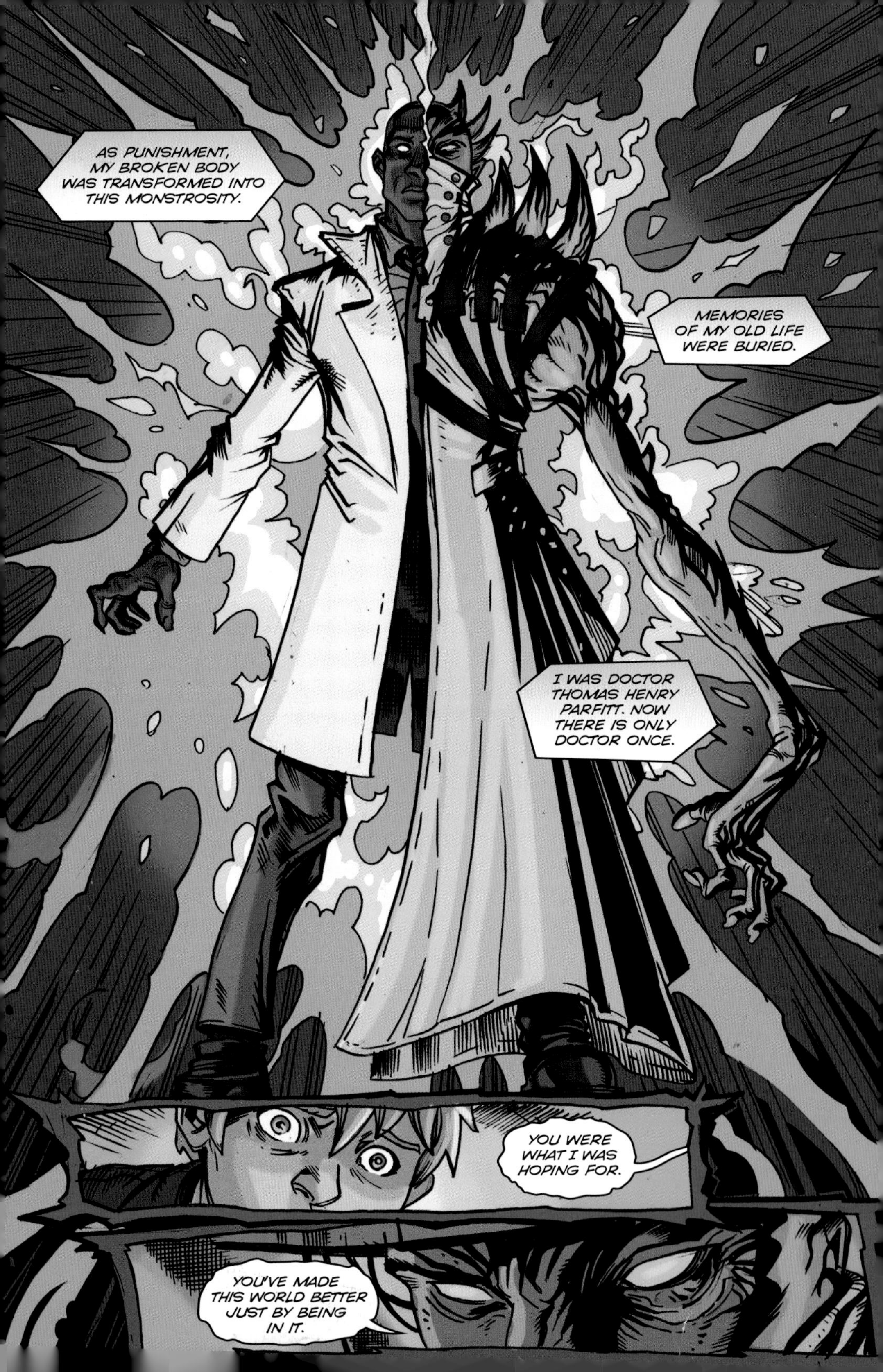
AS PUNISHMENT, MY BROKEN BODY WAS TRANSFORMED INTO THIS MONSTROSITY.
MEMORIES OF MY OLD LIFE WERE BURIED.
I WAS DOCTOR THOMAS HENRY PARFITT. NOW THERE IS ONLY DOCTOR ONCE.
YOU WERE WHAT I WAS HOPING FOR.
YOU'VE MADE THIS WORLD BETTER JUST BY BEING IN IT.

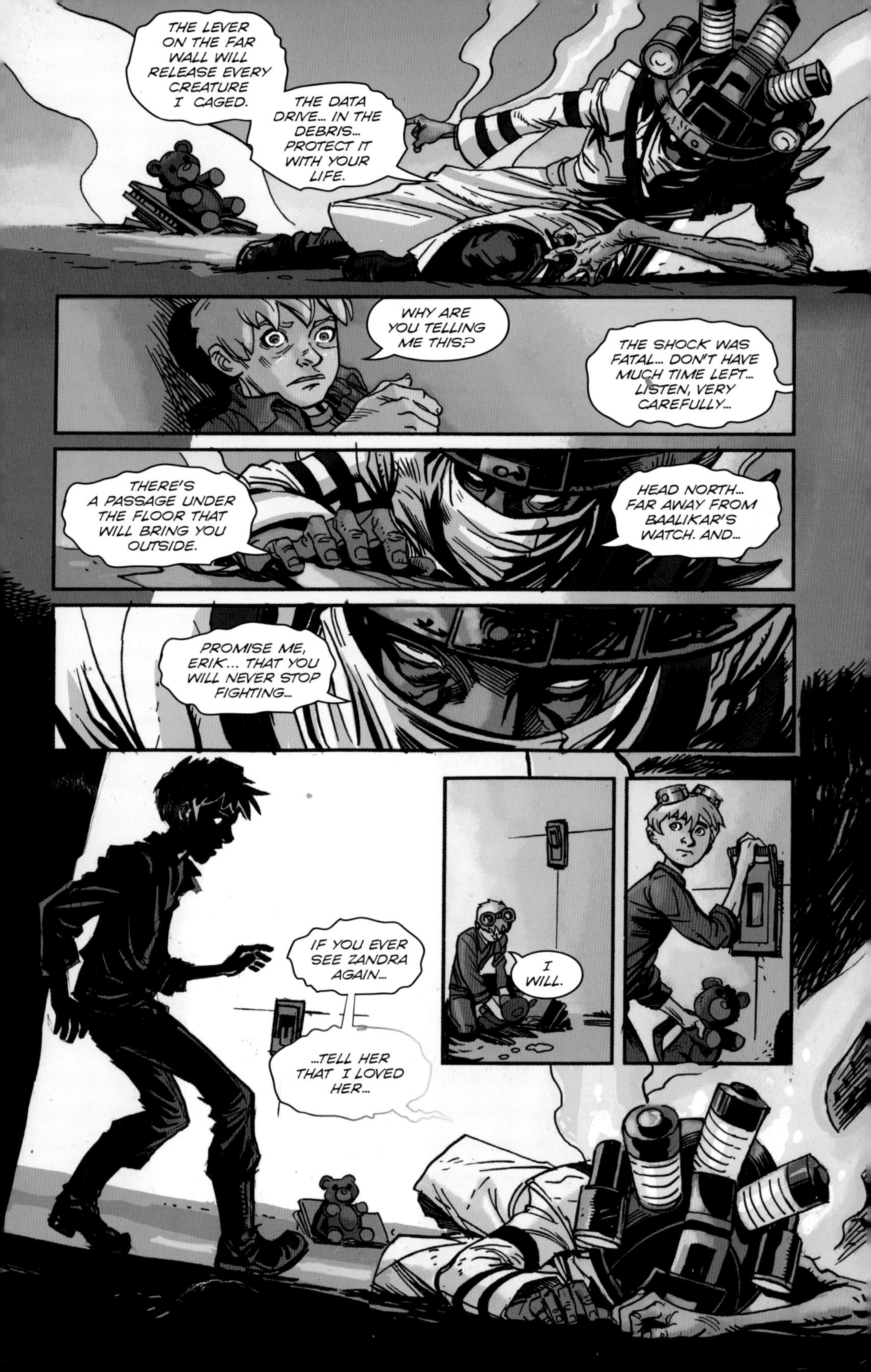
THE LEVER ON THE FAR WALL WILL RELEASE EVERY CREATURE I CAGED.
THE DATA DRIVE... IN THE DEBRIS... PROTECT IT WITH YOUR LIFE.
WHY ARE YOU TELLING ME THIS?
THE SHOCK WAS FATAL... DON'T HAVE MUCH TIME LEFT... LISTEN, VERY CAREFULLY...
THERE'S A PASSAGE UNDER THE FLOOR THAT WILL BRING YOU OUTSIDE.
HEAD NORTH... FAR AWAY FROM BAALIKAR'S WATCH. AND...
PROMISE ME, ERIK... THAT YOU WILL NEVER STOP FIGHTING...
IF YOU EVER SEE ZANDRA AGAIN...
...TELL HER THAT I LOVED HER...
I WILL.

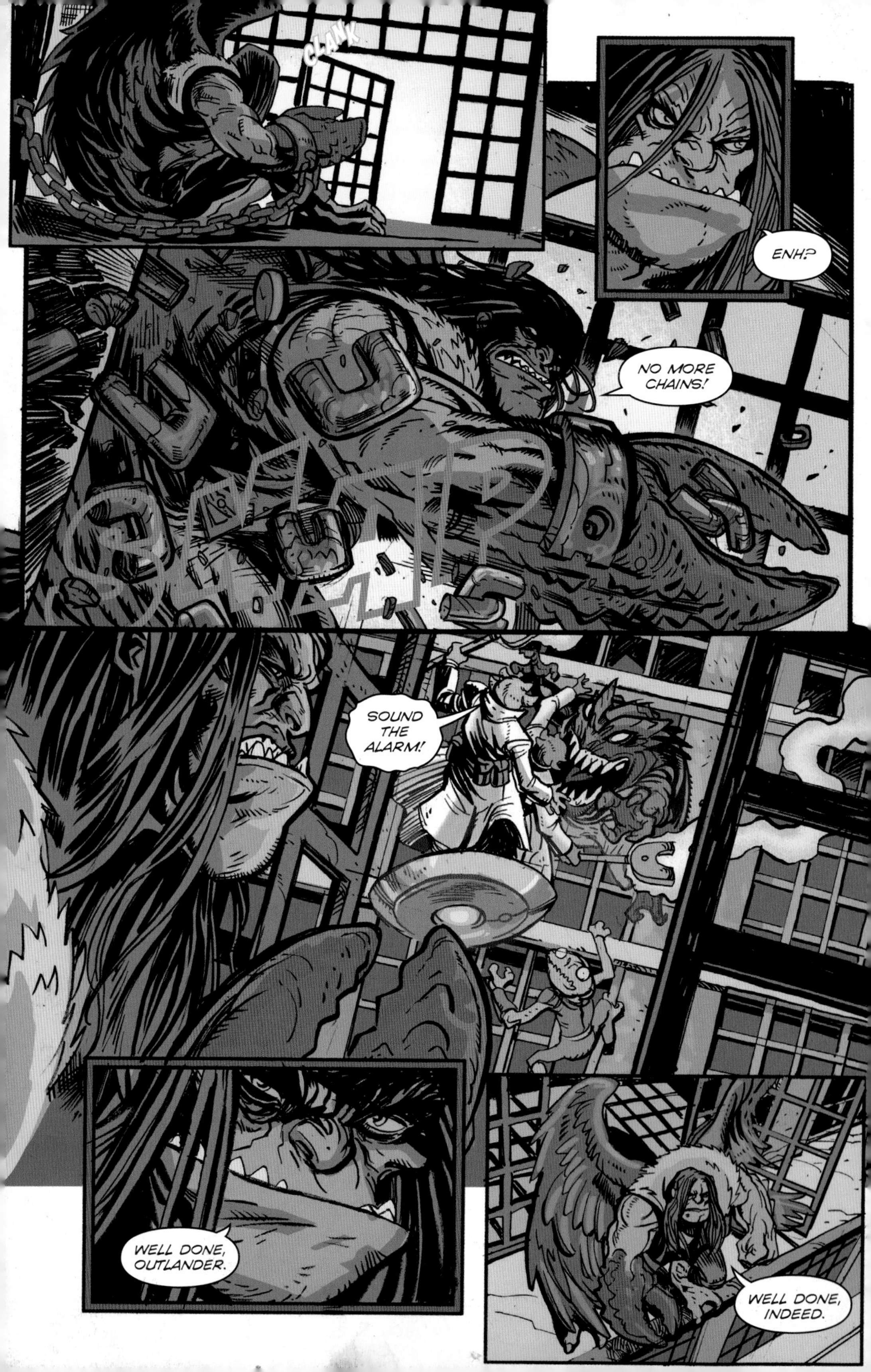
CLANK
ENH?
NO MORE CHAINS!
SOUND THE ALARM!
WELL DONE, OUTLANDER.
WELL DONE, INDEED.

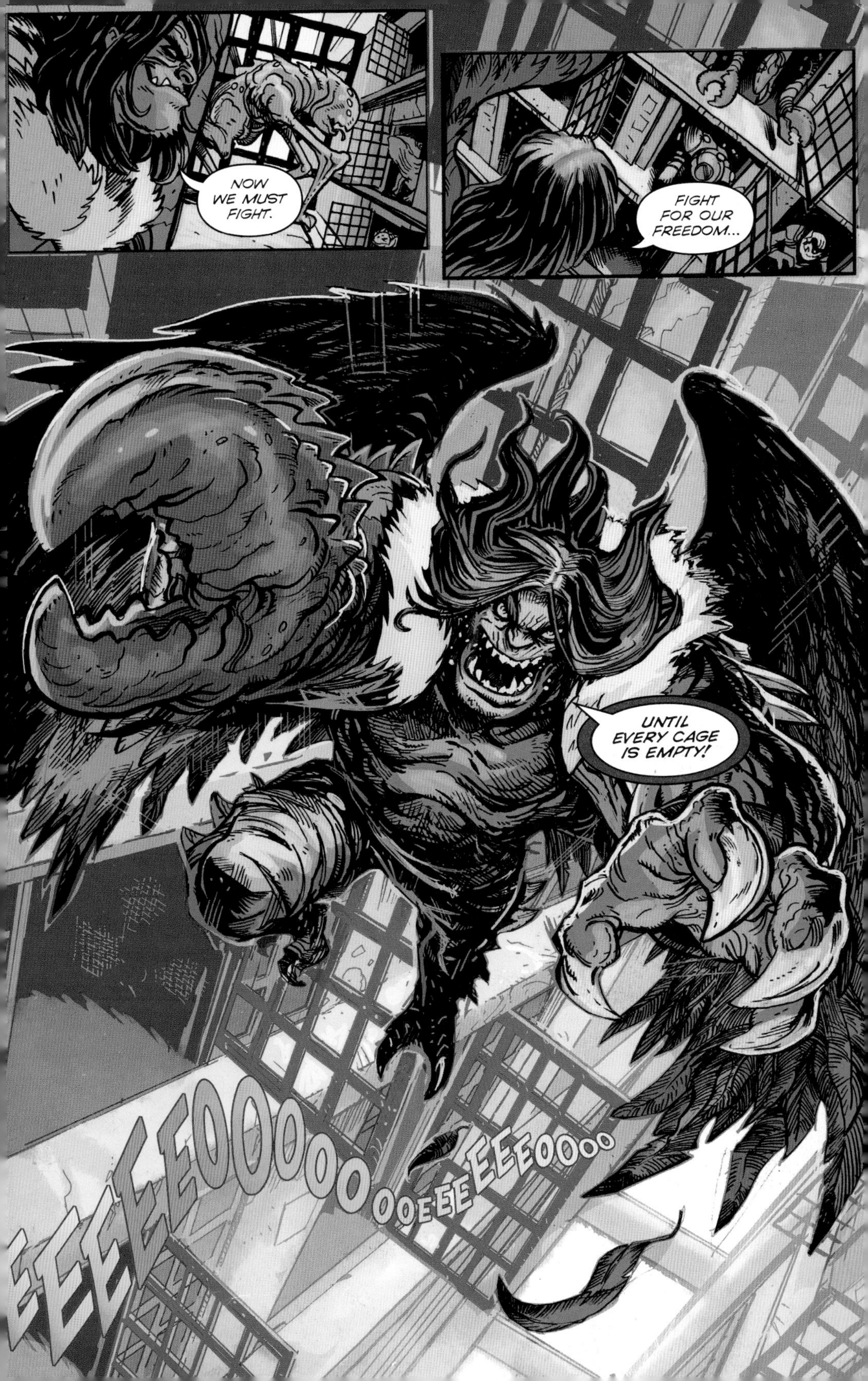
NOW WE MUST FIGHT.
FIGHT FOR OUR FREEDOM...
UNTIL EVERY CAGE IS EMPTY!
EEEEEOOOOOOOOEEEEEOOOO

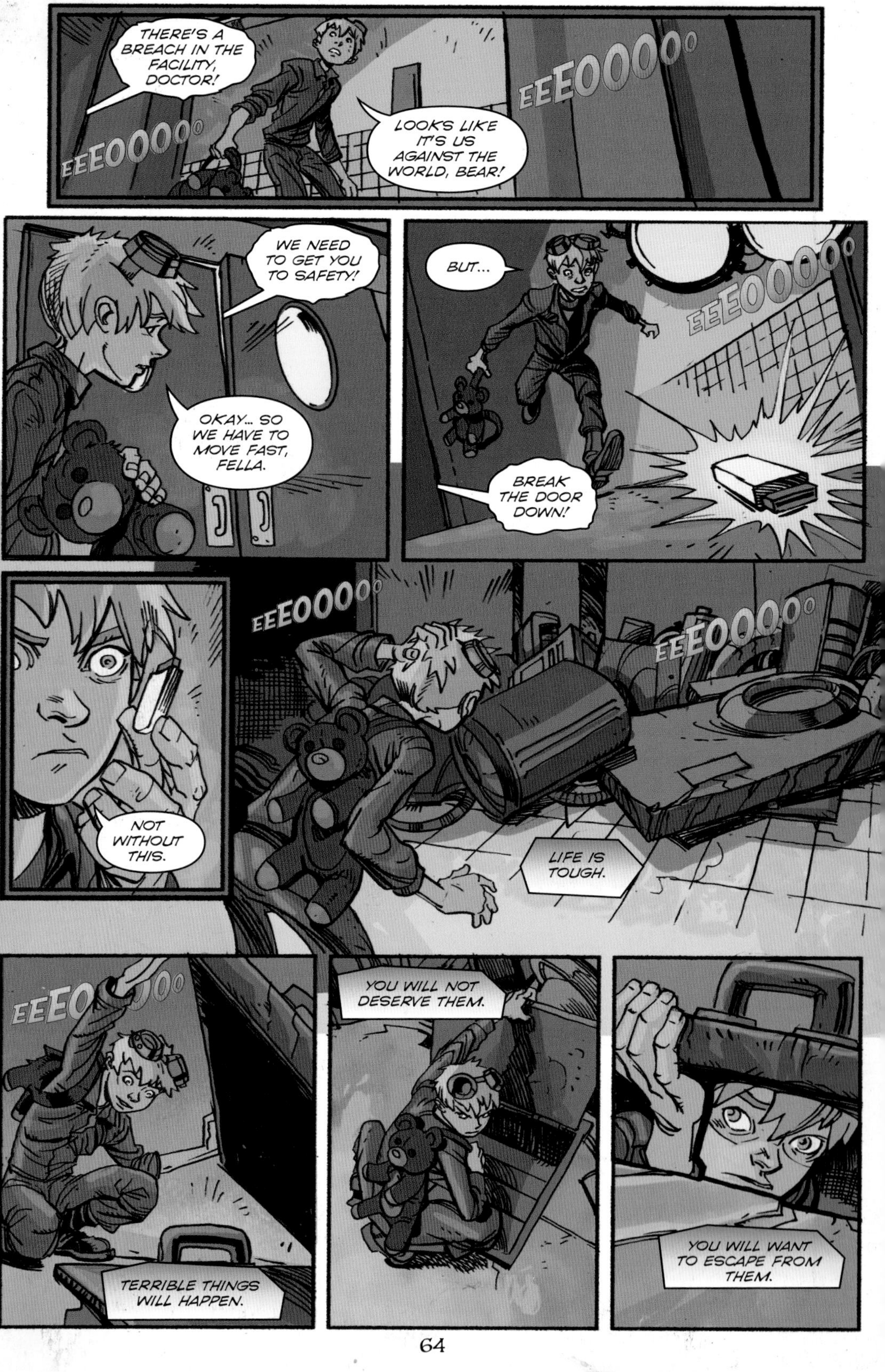
THERE'S A BREACH IN THE FACILITY, DOCTOR!
EEEOOOOo
EEEOOOOo
LOOKS LIKE IT'S US AGAINST THE WORLD, BEAR!
WE NEED TO GET YOU TO SAFETY!
OKAY... SO WE HAVE TO MOVE FAST, FELLA.
BUT...
EEEOOOOOo
BREAK THE DOOR DOWN!
NOT WITHOUT THIS.
EEEOOOOo
EEEOOOOo
LIFE IS TOUGH.
TERRIBLE THINGS WILL HAPPEN.
YOU WILL NOT DESERVE THEM.
YOU WILL WANT TO ESCAPE FROM THEM.

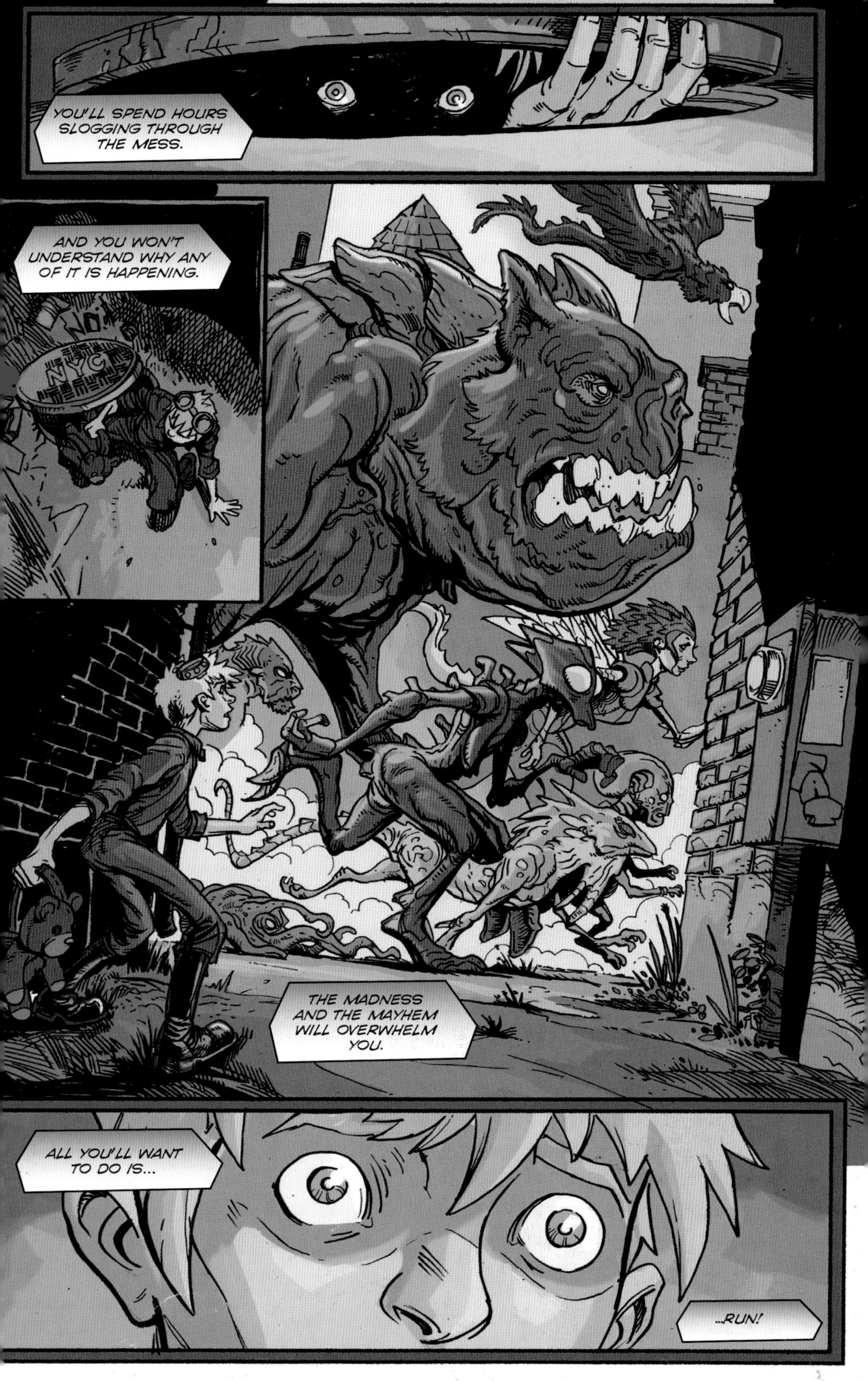
YOU'LL SPEND HOURS SLOGGING THROUGH THE MESS.
AND YOU WON'T UNDERSTAND WHY ANY OF IT IS HAPPENING.
NYC
THE MADNESS AND THE MAYHEM WILL OVERWHELM YOU.
ALL YOU'LL WANT TO DO IS...
...RUN!

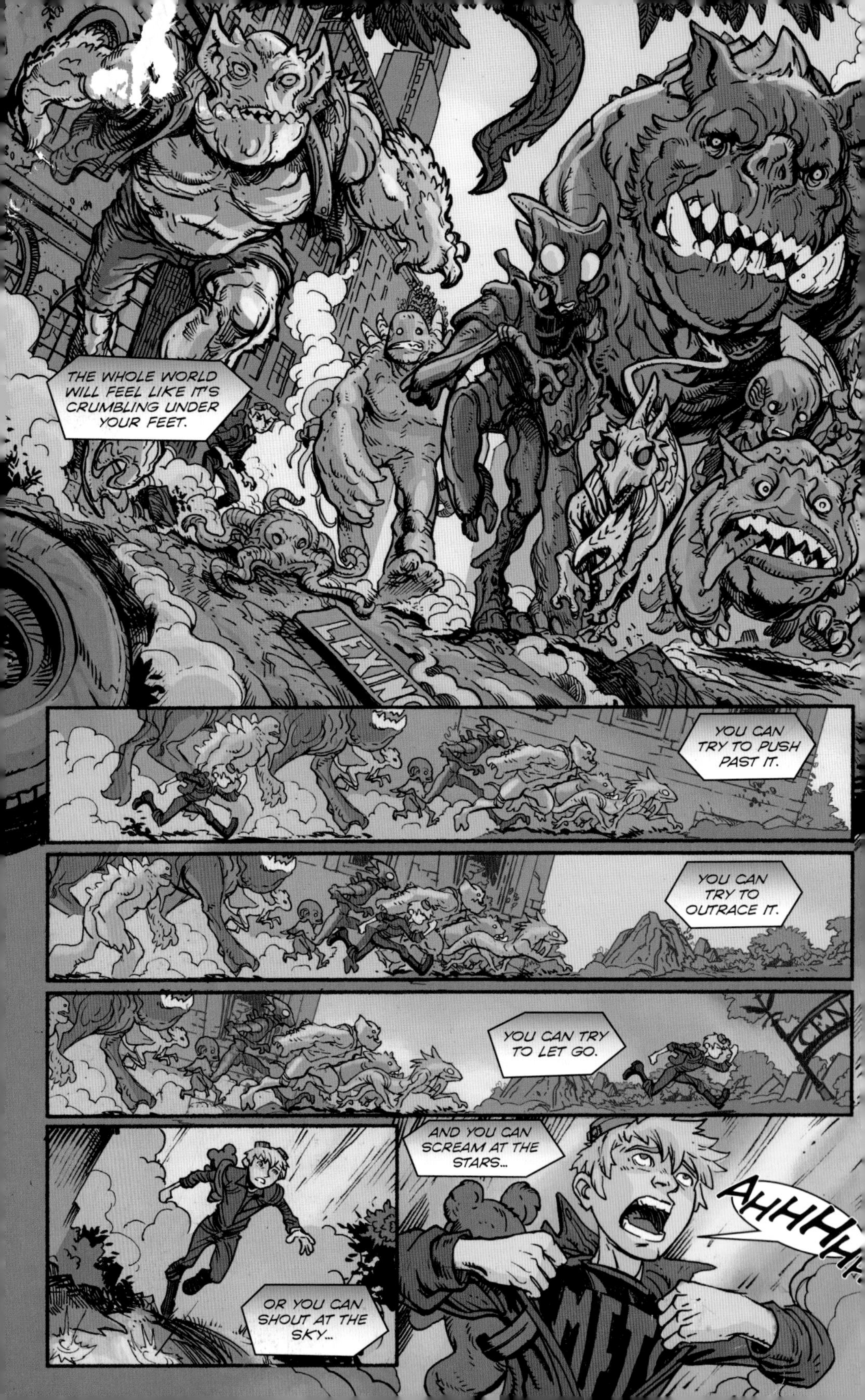
THE WHOLE WORLD WILL FEEL LIKE IT'S CRUMBLING UNDER YOUR FEET.
LEXIN
YOU CAN TRY TO PUSH PAST IT.
YOU CAN TRY TO OUTRACE IT.
YOU CAN TRY TO LET GO.
OR YOU CAN SHOUT AT THE SKY...
AND YOU CAN SCREAM AT THE STARS...
AHHHH

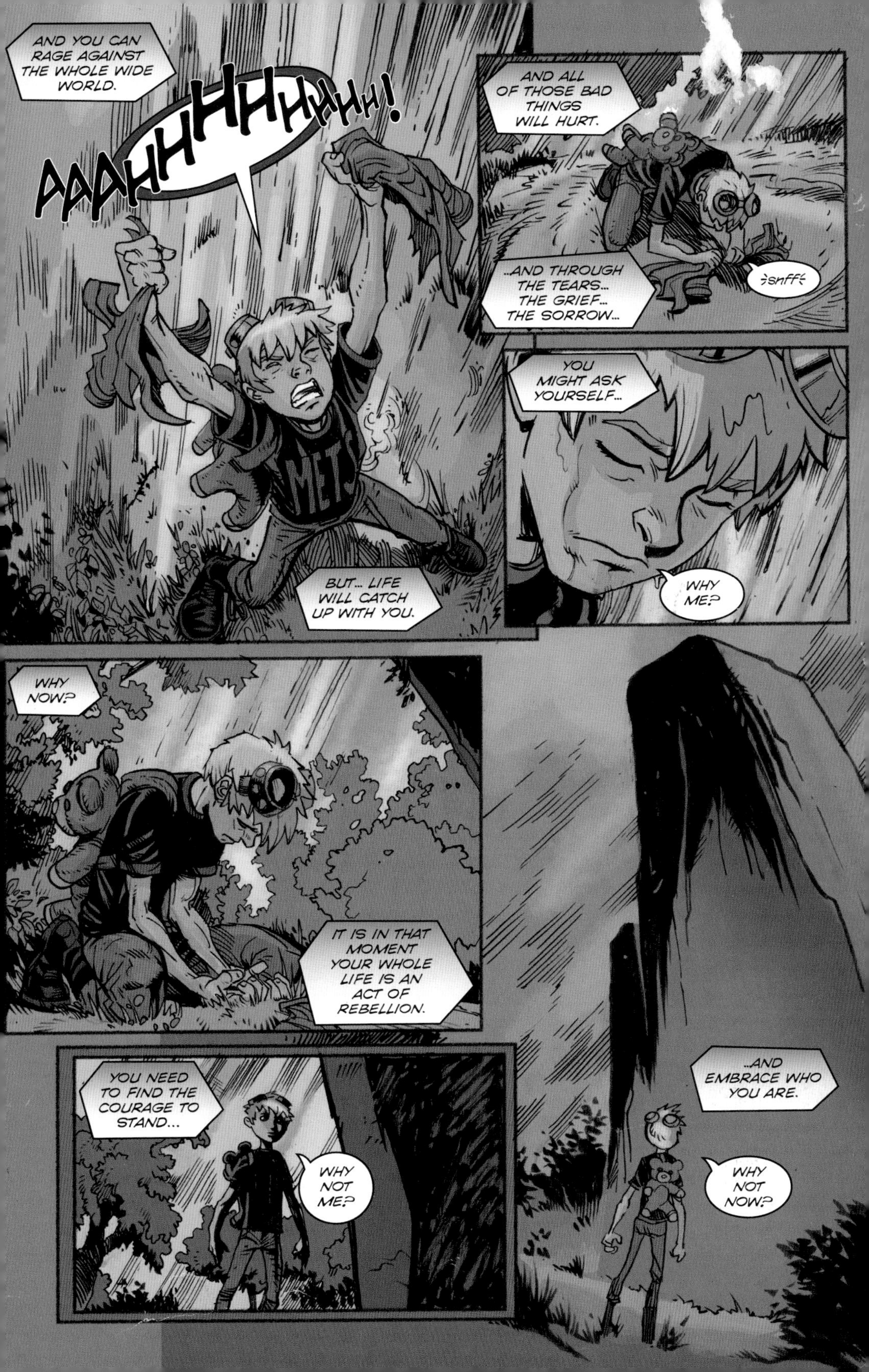
AND YOU CAN RAGE AGAINST THE WHOLE WIDE WORLD.
PAAAHHHHHHHHHH!
BUT... LIFE WILL CATCH UP WITH YOU.
AND ALL OF THOSE BAD THINGS WILL HURT.
...AND THROUGH THE TEARS... THE GRIEF... THE SORROW...
snff
YOU MIGHT ASK YOURSELF...
WHY ME?
WHY NOW?
IT IS IN THAT MOMENT YOUR WHOLE LIFE IS AN ACT OF REBELLION.
YOU NEED TO FIND THE COURAGE TO STAND...
WHY NOT ME?
...AND EMBRACE WHO YOU ARE.
WHY NOT NOW?

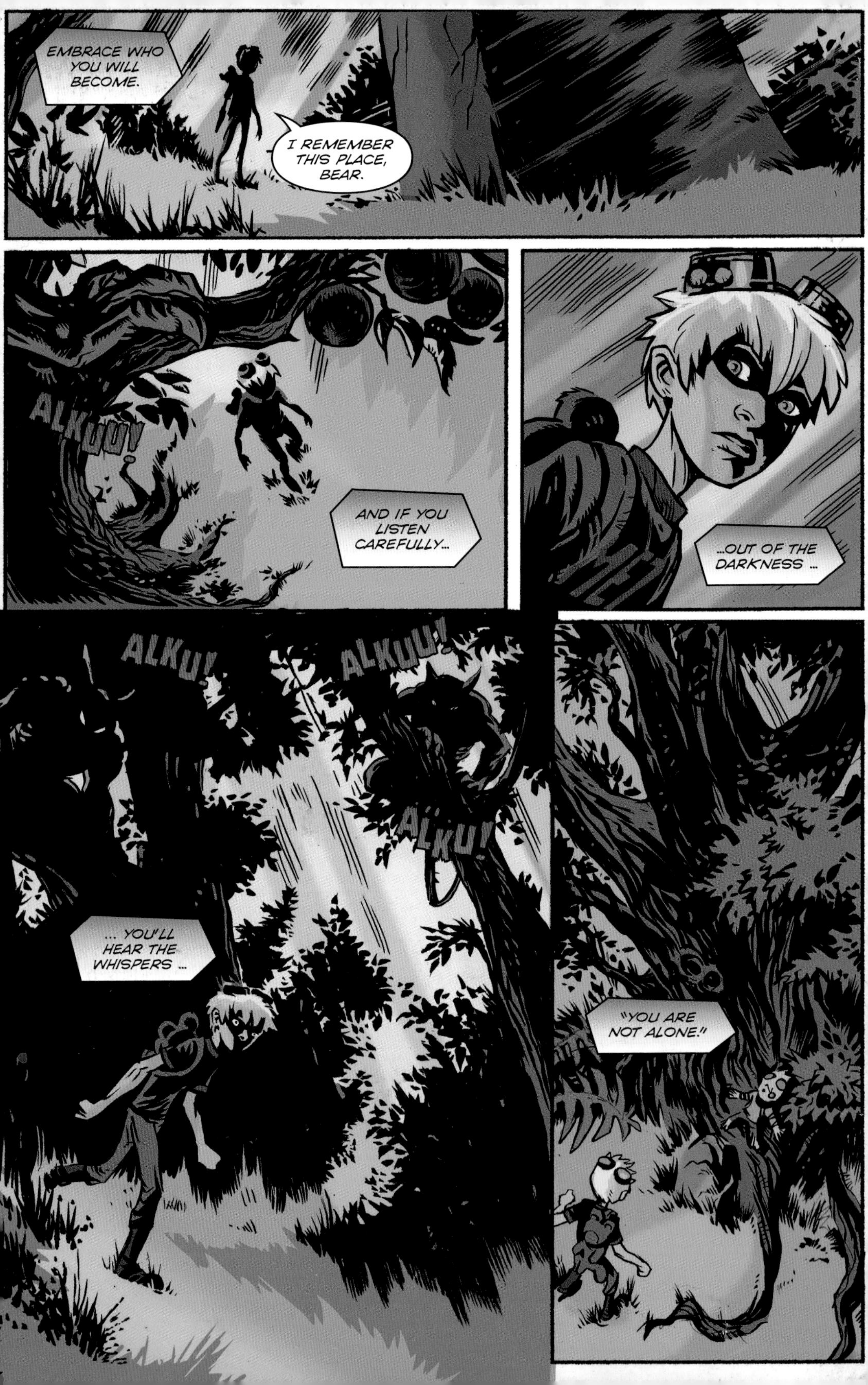
EMBRACE WHO YOU WILL BECOME.
I REMEMBER THIS PLACE, BEAR.
ALKUU!
AND IF YOU LISTEN CAREFULLY...
...OUT OF THE DARKNESS ...
ALKU!
ALKUU!
ALKU!
... YOU'LL HEAR THE WHISPERS ...
"YOU ARE NOT ALONE."

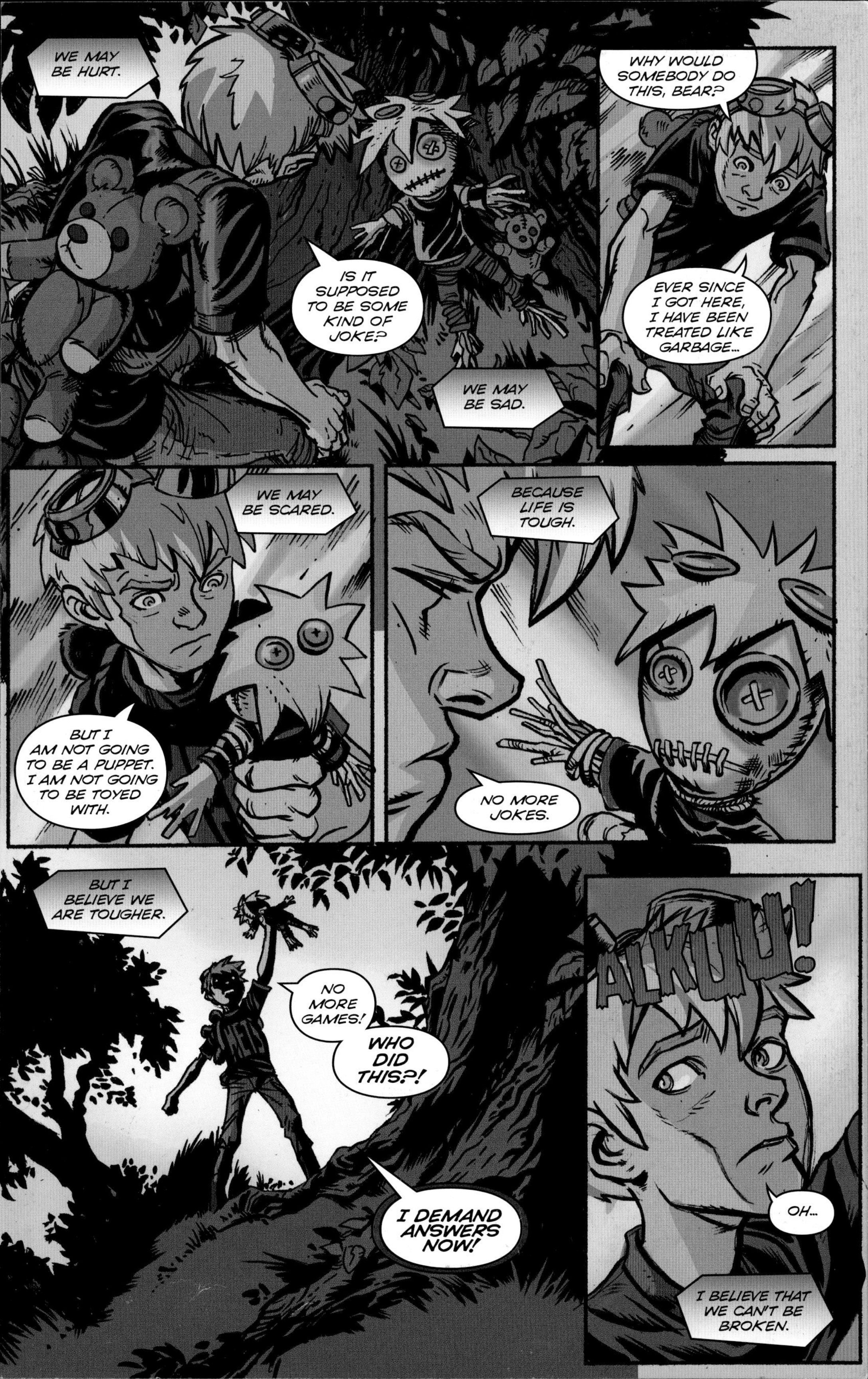
WE MAY BE HURT.
IS IT SUPPOSED TO BE SOME KIND OF JOKE?
WE MAY BE SAD.
WHY WOULD SOMEBODY DO THIS, BEAR?
EVER SINCE I GOT HERE, I HAVE BEEN TREATED LIKE GARBAGE...
WE MAY BE SCARED.
BUT I AM NOT GOING TO BE A PUPPET. I AM NOT GOING TO BE TOYED WITH.
BECAUSE LIFE IS TOUGH.
NO MORE JOKES.
BUT I BELIEVE WE ARE TOUGHER.
NO MORE GAMES!
WHO DID THIS?!
I DEMAND ANSWERS NOW!
ALKUH!
OH...
I BELIEVE THAT WE CAN'T BE BROKEN.

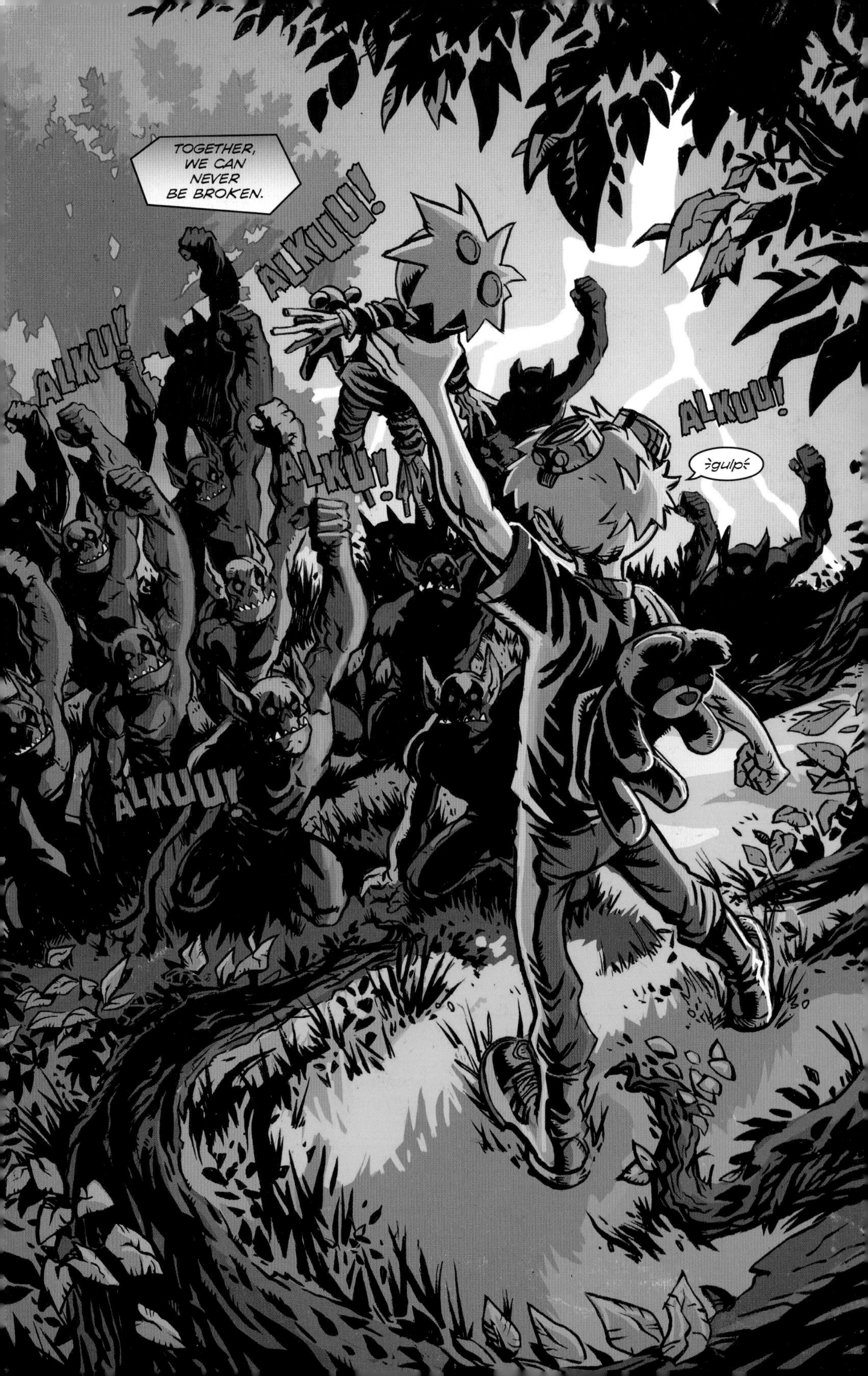
TOGETHER, WE CAN NEVER BE BROKEN.
ALKUU!
ALKU!
ALKU!
ALKUU!
gulp
ALKUU!

WATCH OUT FOR PAPERCUTZ

Welcome to the tangled and twisted third THE ONLY LIVING BOY graphic novel, by David Gallaher and Steve Ellis, from Papercutz–those comicbook geeks dedicated to publishing great graphic novels for all ages. I'm Jim Salicrup, Editor-in-Chief and part-time Comics Publishing Professor, here to reveal a few comicbook basics...

As a long-time comics editor, I've met many intelligent people who've told me that they don't understand comics. That they can't figure out how to read them. Well, today's their lucky day, as the ol' Professor intends to explain it all for you, right here, right now...

First, like most books, you read THE ONLY LIVING BOY from left to right, starting at the top of each page and working your way down. On page 5 of this very graphic novel, Chapter 5 begins with a six-sided box containing four lines of text.

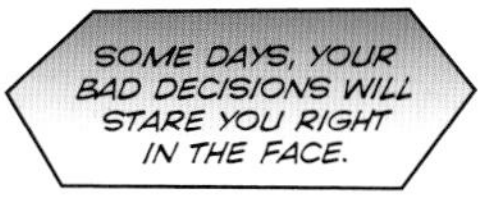
SOME DAYS, YOUR BAD DECISIONS WILL STARE YOU RIGHT IN THE FACE.

Word-filled boxes in comics are called "captions," and provide narration. It could just be an omniscient narrator guiding you through the story, but in this specific case Erik Farrell is telling you his story.

Page 5 is also a full-page illustration enclosed in an even bigger box. Such pages are called "splash pages," as they often try to entice you into reading the rest of the story with some sort of "splashy" visual.

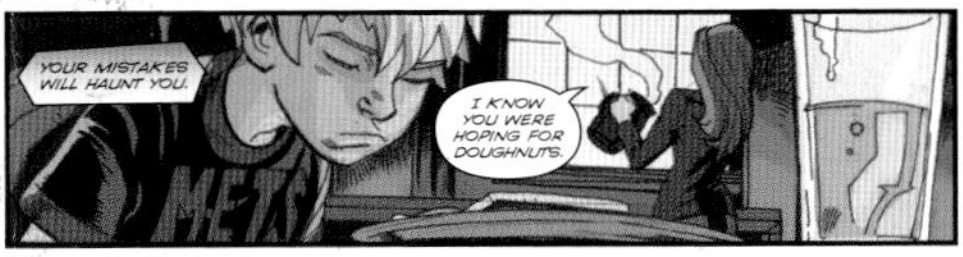
YOUR MISTAKES WILL HAUNT YOU.
I KNOW YOU WERE HOPING FOR DOUGHNUTS.

Page 6 is divided into six sections. Each of those sections, containing words and pictures in a box, is called a "panel." In the first panel, there's another caption revealing Erik's thoughts, and a rounder shape containing more words. Some folks call that round shape a "speech bubble," but serious comicbook people prefer to call it a "word balloon." Don't ask me why a balloon is any more serious than a bubble–I don't know. Jutting out from the top right side of the word balloon is a little nub coming to a point. That's called a "pointer" because it points to the person saying the words within the balloon. Some people call the pointer a "tail," especially when it appears coming from the bottom half of the word balloon, as it looks like, well, a tail.

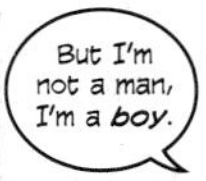
But I'm not a man, I'm a *boy*.

On page 7, panel 7, Erik suddenly speaks in smaller letters that are in upper and lower case–or with capitals and small letters. This is to indicate that he's speaking softly or even whispering.

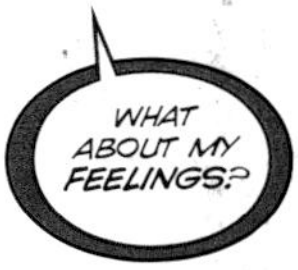
WHAT ABOUT MY FEELINGS?

On page 12, panel 6, an outline appears around Erik's word balloon, this is to indicate Erik is speaking louder, even shouting.

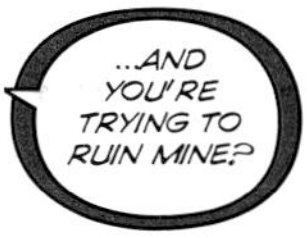
...AND YOU'RE TRYING TO RUIN MINE?

Here's where it gets a little confusing. This balloon with an outline around it as well, is Baalikar's distinctive word balloon. When Baalikar speaks, it's in these balloons.

Big words without any balloon or box containing them are generally describing the sound being created by the action depicted in the artwork. To make up for the lack of sound in comics, "sound effects" were created!

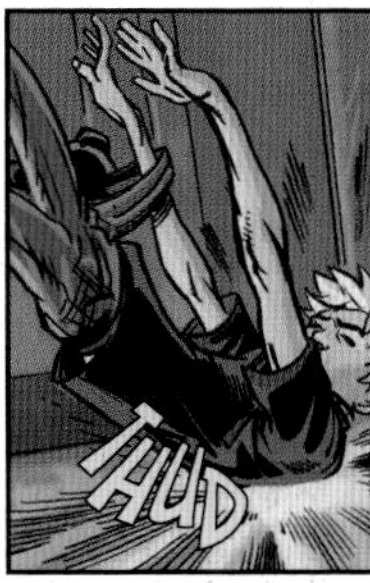
THUD

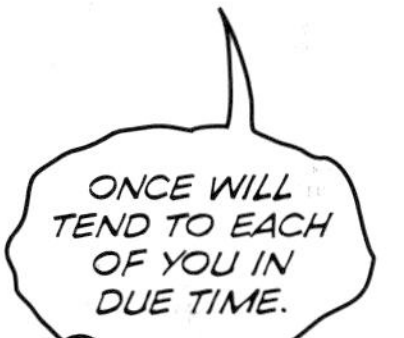
ONCE WILL TEND TO EACH OF YOU IN DUE TIME.

These word balloons with a wavy outline are the distinctive word balloons for Doctor Once.

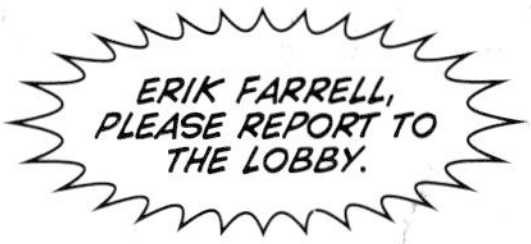
ERIK FARRELL, PLEASE REPORT TO THE LOBBY.

This word balloon with an outline composed entirely of pointy bits is sometimes called an "electric balloon," used to indicate sound coming from electrical devices such as radios and TVs. In this case the voice is coming from a Public Address system.

And that's about it! If you're able to understand the complex science fiction elements of Chapter 6, we doubt you'll have any trouble understanding these basic elements of comic-book storytelling. If you do have any questions, feel free to contact me at the addresses indicated below. So, until we meet again in THE ONLY LIVING BOY #4 "Through the Murky Deep," class dismissed!

Thanks, Jim

STAY IN TOUCH!

EMAIL:	salicrup@papercutz.com
WEB:	papercutz.com
TWITTER:	@papercutzgn
FACEBOOK:	PAPERCUTZGRAPHICNOVELS
FAN MAIL:	Papercutz, 160 Broadway, Suite 700, East Wing, New York, NY 10038

COMING SOON!

THE ONLY LIVING BOY
PRISONER OF THE PATCHWORK PLANET
PAPERCUTZ

THE ONLY LIVING BOY #1

THE ONLY LIVING BOY
BEYOND SEA AND SKY
PAPERCUTZ

THE ONLY LIVING BOY #2

THE ONLY LIVING BOY
ONCE UPON A TIME
PAPERCUTZ

THE ONLY LIVING BOY #3

THE ONLY LIVING BOY
THROUGH THE MURKY DEEP
PAPERCUTZ

THE ONLY LIVING BOY #4

THE ONLY LIVING BOY

"A modern masterpiece for all ages. I wish more comics were like this."
-Jimmy Palmiotti, writer, *Harley Quinn, Futurama*

"Scaly monsters, alien heroines, giant evil dragons, underground cities, secrets–this is adventuresome, fast-paced alternate-reality action with engaging, layered characters and great, great drawing. Everything you could possibly want in a comic, really."
-Nick Abadzis, author of *Laika*

THE ONLY LIVING BOY graphic novels are available for $8.99 in paperback, and $13.99 in hardcover. Available from booksellers everywhere. You can also order online from www.papercutz.com. Or call 1-800-886-1223, Monday through Friday, 9–5 EST. MC, Visa, and AmEx accepted. To order by mail, please add $4.00 for postage and handling for first book ordered, $1.00 for each additional book and make check payable to NBM Publishing. Send to: Papercutz, 160 Broadway, Suite 700, East Wing, New York, NY 10038.

THE ONLY LIVING BOY graphic novels are also available wherever e-books are sold.

PAPERCUTZ™
Papercutz.com